THE FEUDERS

BY

TERRY MAY

ROCK HILL PUBLISHING

Published by: Rock Hill Publishing

ISBN: 978-0-9831817-3-6

For Howard, David, Marisa and Philip

CHAPTER 1

Cloud won the fight.

But there was something strange about the look on the other man's face when he danced into center ring after the bell, hands too low, head unprotected. His moves were different. Cloud backed up, tried to figure it out. He saw the boxer's eyes turn up as though in prayer, saw his face go white and his arms throw out sideways like he was nailed to a cross. And fall like that. All faster than you could catch a deep breath.

The referee went down on a knee, then rose up and yelled, "O'Keefe ain't breathing." The men gathered in the St. Louis alley came alive at that, calling out at one another so loud you could barely hear it when the referee said, "Tom Cloud takes it, boys."

Somebody put money in his hand and left it there, the winner's purse, blood from his hand dripping onto the greenbacks, his fingers numb, his knuckles skinned and scabbed from this one and the other fights of the last two weeks. But he was not supposed to win this way. Nobody had died before.

He heard a woman scream, a high-pitched sound that bounced off the brick walls on either side. She came through the crowd of men in a flowered dress and a hat with lace on it, kneeling beside the fallen boxer, but looking up at Cloud, eyes wide and wet. He kept thinking she would mouth some accusation, but she only stared for a moment and turned back to the fallen fighter, laid a hand on his bruised face and patted it twice as though offering comfort. Men lifted her away and Cloud stood there rooted and waiting, feeling like he might never move again.

Three level heads from the sporting crowd got him safe to his hotel room, helped him pack his clothes in the draw-string sack he used, then walked him to the docks with a ticket for New Orleans on the riverboat *Natchez*.

The ticket paid for bunk space, but he spent most of the four nights and five days on deck. It was hot on the boat, even with the wind off the river, though it was people kept him away. He went down for a meal or two each day, avoiding eyes and conversation. At night he spread a blanket on the hard decking and watched the stars, sometimes hearing nightbirds along the banks, smelling the muddy river and the musk of spray off the turning wheel.

On the last night a man came to stand over him and lit a cigar, flipped the match at the rail and said, "We been wondering why you don't join us for a hand of poker." He was a tall man, well-built, in a satin coat and a high hat and his inquiry had an edge in it.

"Thanks, anyway," Tom said.

"Too good for us, I guess."

"Not at all, mister. Just don't feel like it."

The stranger pulled a deep drag off his cigar and blew the smoke upward at the stars then walked away.

Tom was surprised at the stiffness in the muscles of his face and the tremor in his hands. And at the sudden, rapid beating of his heart.

CHAPTER 2

He felt just then the way he'd always felt before battle, one gray dot in a sea of soldiers, two weary legs and a Springfield musket. The Army of Tennessee, friends and neighbors, gray waves of angry men taking minié balls in the chest and falling into their private peace.

He'd learned to use his fists in the camps between battles, matched up against others. Something for the officers to bet their wages on in the absence of racing horses. And he had always won, noticed how eyes followed him with what he took for admiration, made sergeant by his twenty-first birthday, all because of the scabbed hands that trembled now at the displeasure of a Mississipi dandy.

Like most soldiers at war he had killed other men, some at a distance, some up close, and always gone on to the next man, the next battle with a clear head and clean heart. But the man back in St. Louis stayed with him. He tried to shake O'keefe out of his mind, but the big redhead wouldn't go, circling in Cloud's thoughts as he'd circled in the ring, face wary and smart, hands high and ready, until the end of it when his arms shot out and spit slid between his lips. The worst of it was how his eyes had turned up like he was looking for a way to fly out of that alley til his knees went and the rest of him poured down like water.

O'Keefe, like many opponents, had come in quick expecting no fight from a tall, slender man like Tom Cloud. Most went staggering back surprised at the power in him. Many a time, that's as far as the fight went—a quick rush, a roundhouse right from Cloud and the other fellow on his back. Gamblers who'd bet on him liked that. People who'd come to watch a good fight didn't.

7

This fight hadn't gone that way. O'Keefe had been surprised, all right, but he'd stayed on his feet and kept coming. Cloud had the reach on him, and used it, throwing fists til somebody hit the bell, then stepping out for the second round and watching helpless as the bad thing happened—the bad thing stuck in his head now like a scared bird wanting out.

CHAPTER 3

In New Orleans he posted a letter back to the Tennessee farm, remembering his boyhood in the country east of Nashville and hoped it got there. He figured it would; these Yankees seemed like they got things done right since they took over. One of the things they might do now was chase him to the ends of the earth on account of that dead man back in St. Louis. No way to know without asking and he didn't intend asking. Thing to do was give it time, then maybe someday get himself home to that place of soft mornings and sweet memories.

He felt smaller and everything around him seemed larger than before. As it advised in the Bible at the bottom of his sack, he was in the world but not of it.

A man who looked like he'd seen it all and didn't like any of it walked with him behind a horse stable and pointed to an animal.

"You could do worse than that one."

"I'll have to look him over." Already knowing he wouldn't buy the horse, too polite to say so. The dappled gray gelding had a pinched look about him, chest too thin, legs poorly fashioned. From over his shoulder another voice.

"You'd be a fool to buy that wolfbait, friend."

A short man in a stained stetson looked up at him from under the brim of it. A man freshly barbered from the scent, wearing new clothes and knee-high boots with a new shine. The stable man didn't seem bothered by the intrusion. "Back yonder tied at the gate is the best bargain you'll ever run across."

"Your horse?"

"I wouldn't be offering you somebody else's, would I?" Whether it was a challenge or a joke Tom Cloud couldn't say.

Cloud glanced over at the stable man and got a shrug from him. "Go on and look."

The stranger walked in front of him like one of the Bantam roosters his father kept on the Nashville farm. *banties,* they called them. Not enough meat to make a meal on, but something encouraging about the walk.

The reddest strawberry roan Cloud had ever seen stared back at him. A cow pony by appearance, well-formed head with a white blaze. The saddle cinched on him looked like it had come through a brier patch.

"Ain't selling my rig, though."

Cloud nodded, going though the motions of checking the roan out, knowing all along that it was a good, sound animal in front of him, wondering what he ought to offer.

He heard the stable man say, "You from that Texas crowd?"

"Yessir. Headed back in a few hours."

"Decided on a boat ride, I guess."

It was strange hearing the two men talk, the trader's voice soft as a song, the Texan's more like those he was used to hearing in Tennessee, but with more curl in the tongue, a sharper sting in the ears.

"Yessir. I'm takin' the *Mary* to Galveston. And I'll pay your commission if he wants my horse. Fair's fair."

"Same story I done heard from plenty of the crew you come out here with. Them's they horses back there, the ones I got for sale. I'll take yours, too, this man don't want him."

Tom looked at the banty rooster. "I was thinking I might aim for Texas myself."

Slow to respond, the cowboy took off his Stetson and scratched at his head, his fresh haircut plain for anybody to see. "You'd do best to aim by boat, friend, despite me losing a sale. Can't help being honest. Mama taught me too good."

"Hard journey?"

"You could call it that. I just helped push three thousand head here to market, and I think it's the last one comin' this direction. We'll be goin' north to the railroad from now on, or maybe down to San Antone, and I say good for us."

CHAPTER 4

Put into service that same year, *The Mary* was so new Tom could smell her paint. The cabin he shared with Landis Tarver was the nicest place he'd ever slept, and the iron-hulled steamer smoothed the Gulf waves all the way to the port at Galveston Island. Another half-dozen cowhands, the bunch Lanny had come out with on the cattle drive, were on the boat, but it was a quiet ride. They were all tired from the drive, or more likely from the good times in New Orleans after they drew their wages.

Tarver liked sharing his opinions.

"Down here we went from bein' Mexicans to bein' Texicans, then rebels and now we're back in the Union again. For good or bad I don't know. Mostly I'm just surprised I lived through the conflagration and still draw breath."

Tom listened and held on to his own words like they were gold.

"You can ride this boat as far as Corpus Christi if you want to, and there's others go up the Rio Grande into the nueces strip. You know the country?"

"Not a bit," Tom told him.

"For my money the strip's a good place to stay away from for now. Thorns and Mexican raiders cooked up with Comanches and Lipans is too much adventure for my taste."

"You worked out there?"

"No, you got King and Kennedy on big spreads hire mostly Mexican vaqueros and there's a few small holdings that get rustled and massacred on a regular basis. Hard to spend your money with your scalp gone."

"I hear the eastern half is peaceful."

13

"It is, I reckon. Got some Indians, mostly peaceful, got some farmers and timber cutters. You like handling a crosscut saw, that's where I'd head."

He remembered the years he spent helping clear the Nashville farm.

"Mister Cloud, you got a pistol in that sack?"

"Why?"

"Well, I'm a curious man and I don't want to get shot for askin' questions you don't like."

"You'll have to loan me yours, I guess. I got nothing to shoot you with."

The little man laughed. "Comes to that, it's in that saddlebag yonder where you seen me put it. I'll take the chance, though; we're close enough to land I could swim it if I needed to get away from you. What kind of work you do? No offense intended."

"I don't mind. Well, I've farmed and I've soldiered, and that about covers it." The rest best forgotten.

Tarver chewed on the news. "Either one ought to be a help to you out here. You can ride, I guess, seein' you was gonna buy a horse. You know cows?"

"Not the way you mean, no. Why?"

"No reason. Well-spoke as you are I had you figured for a lawyer."

"My mother taught school between crops."

"Well, that eases my mind. I'd hate to make a friend that turned out to be a lawyer. I'll offer a little advice to you if you care to hear it, otherwise I'll shut my mouth."

"Go ahead."

"If you ain't got a pistol in that sack, buy one or steal it, and a good Bowie knife, too. I won't say for sure that you'll need 'em, but it's very likely."

"I planned on it, but thanks."

"If you want to ferry over to the mainland with me I'll show you where you can get what you need."

CHAPTER 5

They docked a day later among five acres of cotton bales upright as soldiers standing side by side at attention. A ferry boat was ready to leave, but it was crowded and they waited for the next one, taking up the time by walking a few streets. Galveston had surprised Tom. It was a real city, big houses, stores, all kinds of businesses, ocean-going ships anchored in the Gulf. The air smelled like clothes washed fresh and hung on a line to dry in the sun. Like all cowhands, Lanny didn't like walking and said so. They took the next one across.

Tom said, "You talked about cattle, but you didn't tell me about cotton. They farm a lot of it here?"

The little man nodded a yes. "In the Brazos valley and up along the Trinity." He braced himself against the ferry rail, his saddle and the rest of his rigging on the deck at his feet, looking back at the island. He pulled a snuff can out of his back pocket and poured a helping under his lip, then put the can back while he worked his mouth on the cud.

Before Tom got a longer answer a man in rough range clothes and a flat-crowned straw hat came up to them and took hold of Lanny's arm.

"I didn't know you was here, Rudy."

The man glanced at Tom and put has attention back on Lanny. He was older, looked like he'd been on the fire longer than the other cowhands Tom had met, cooked to a finer turn.

"New friend of mine, Rudy. Tom Cloud from Tennessee. Tom, this's Rudolph Sterns. He's ramrod on the Bigboy, where I'm workin'."

Sterns took his hand off Lanny's arm and reached out to shake the one Tom offered. The man's grip was hard enough to hurt Tom's knuckles, not quite healed and tender still. The older man said to Lanny, "That Jones boy stayed in New Orleans. Found him a girl, I think. Now old Pinky's changed his mind and headed back out to Albuquerque, so I'm short two hands for winter. You still plan to stay on, don't you?"

"Count on me, Rudy. What about some of them other boys?"

"No, everybody's done planned to go somewheres else. I'll look around Houston, maybe find a couple."

Lanny glanced at Tom, left it open for him, left it for him to speak up, but Tom had given no thought to what he really wanted to do. He had some money, but it wouldn't take long to spend it all if he wasn't careful. Maybe a job was the right thing until he got his bearings.

Sterns had turned to walk away before Tom made up his mind and spoke out. "What about me?" He said.

CHAPTER 6

The sign over the door said *ARMORER,* and the store inside was filled with guns, something he'd never seen before. In Cloud's experience, you found weapons strapped on dead men or for sale behind the counter of a general store next to beans and flour. *Armorer.* Funny thing to call a gun shop. It smelled like oil and brass inside.

A skinny fellow in a red and white striped shirt and blue suspenders didn't look all that happy they'd come in. "Gents," he said, in an English accent, and waited.

Lanny Tarver said, "My pardner here's in need of a sidearm."

The man lowered his voice like he was telling a secret. "I have something just come in no more than an hour ago, off the steamer *Mary.*" Tom noticed a wooden crate next to a back counter, the top prised off with the hammer that still lay on top of it.

Lanny said, "Must've made the trip on the boat with us."

The red and white striped arm dipped into the crate and came out with the scariest looking pistol Tom Cloud had ever seen.

"This 'ere's the new Colt, Gents. *Peacemaker,* some calls it. Holds a .45 caliber metal cartridge. Stop a bull elyphant it will. Every man you know will be wanting one."

"You got the shells to go with it?" Lanny said.

The man didn't reply, just pointed to another crate not yet opened.

The price was more than Cloud wanted to pay, but he dickered and got it down a few dollars. Lanny passed on it.

"This old .44 of mine will do a while yet, as fine looking as that new one is. Maybe Santy Clause will bring me one at Christmas time."

After paying for the pistol, and the Bowie knife Lanny had talked him into, *you'll thank me one of these days,* Cloud felt a big hole in his finances. He'd already paid for the horse and the outfit to go with it, and a pair of high-heeled boots and a hat like the little rooster wore, plus a canvas coat. He hoped they'd reached the end of the buying spree.

"Would you be wanting a long gun as well?"

He glanced at Lanny and got no hint of what his answer ought to be. "No, this'll do for now." They rode out of town side by side, a few hours before dark

Leather. The perfume of it was all around him, off the new holster strapped to his left hip the way Lanny had showed him, off the cartridge belt, saddle and bridle, all honey-brown in their newness, all creaky as an old rocking chair. And the boots, too. He liked the smell, and liked the salty musk of horse sweat that rose off the pony Lanny's friend had called a *Silver Grullo.*

Lanny said, "You got a good mount there, Tom. Could you tell old Charley was glad to see me?" He ran his fingers through the mane on his horse's neck.

"Well, he was glad to see that sugar in your pocket."

"Naw, he's my buddy. Ain't you, Charley? I've had 'im five years now and never goin' to part with 'im. Stays in George's pasture every year while I go on a drive. Watches for me til I come back."

Cloud had been a hard sell to the ranch boss, but Lanny had put his word on the line, promised Sterns he'd teach Tom all he'd need to know. The job didn't sound hard, riding the southwest line partnered with Lanny Tarver. Main thing was to keep the herd from straying off toward Mexico.

"The other thing," Lanny had said later, "Is to keep Mexico from strayin' into the herd."

CHAPTER 7

Tom liked the way the other man rode, elbows close in to the sides of his body, right hand free and ready for anything, reins loose in his left, his back straight, hips moving with the bay cowpony's gait. He tried it himself, and the grullo picked up a little speed. It seemed to help the animal's movement.

"How far is the ranch? And what did you call it? The Bigboy?" They were headed into a showy sunset building on clouds at the horizon.

"Yeah. Over on the other side of the Colorado River. We'll stop off and camp on the Brazos tonight and it's another day's ride. Headquarters is on the southern edge of our range, and it goes up nearly to the lost pines."

"Every time you answer a question you raise up a new one."

"Bigboy's what everybody calls it, but it's the BB, owner's named Billy Barnett. Billy is about ten feet tall and outweighs your pony."

"I hope you don't offend easy, but that sounds a little exaggerated to me."

Tarver laughed. "Maybe a little, but don't act surprised if you ever meet him."

"Don't he live there?"

"Some, but he's got a big house up in Austin he stays at mostly."

"What did you say about pines?"

"These that we're in now peter out a ways up and there's a sort of island of 'em around Bastrop that's cut off by oaks and such. Everybody calls 'em the lost pines. The Bigboy's mostly blackland prairie and oak and elm. Mesquite, too, but it's lots easier workin' cows on it compared to the brush country down south."

The sunset went from rose to gray, and shaded off into black in the next few hours. There were flocks of seagulls in the sky, and lonely white birds with long wings that raised a feeling of homesickness and yearning in Tom. He shook it off again and again, but it stayed with him. The smell of salt water eased off in the early night and the horses snorted at uncertain shadows beside the road. Cloud's legs were starting to hurt from the unaccustomed ride when he saw a light flickering ahead.

"Campfire?"

"Yeah. We're nearly to the river. We can go up and stay with them people if you want to, or make camp on our own."

Tom hadn't lost the yearning. "Go ahead if you want to. Probably friends of yours. I'm not in the mood for company, myself."

Lanny swung his horse to the right and said, "Follow me. I know a good spot."

They made coffee over a fire built on wood Tom cut with his new knife, and unwrapped the bread and dried beef from town. Bullfrogs and alligators sounded from the river.

"I guess there's plenty of snakes out here."

"There is, and every blamed kind you ever heard of. Watch where you step."

They finished off the food and Lanny packed fresh snuff under his lip before they rolled up in their blankets to get away from the mosquitoes. Their horses grazed outside the light from the fire, snorting now and then at some imagined threat, or maybe a traveling water moccasin. Tom was a little surprised to notice the lonesome feeling had lifted and his eyes had grown heavy in the flicker of firelight that peeped through the weave of cloth.

A second later, it seemed, he heard two gunshots close together. He thought at first it was a Yankee attack, threw off his blanket, too frightened to notice the cooler air of morning, remembered where he was and tried to find the new revolver, then saw Lanny Tarver coming out of the woods with a rifle in one hand and two squirrels in the other. Daylight wasn't much more than a promise yet. He smelled rain and the ashes of the fire, the faint and familiar scent of burned gunpowder.

"Rise and shine. I'll skin out these tree rats if you'll freshen that fire."

It didn't take either man long to get his chores done, and they ate roasted squirrel meat and drank hot coffee and Tom began to feel better about the morning. The fresh smell of rain was getting stronger, coming on a wind from the east. The marshland around them gave off a stink of mud and sluggish water that put him in mind of places he'd bivouacked on the Mississippi.

Lanny got a new dip of snuff in place and said, "I'll go find the transportation. We need to get away from that rain shower."

They walked the horses across a shallow ford that sucked at the animal's hoofs and trotted northwest toward drier ground. From his groin to his knees both legs were so sore Tom gritted his teeth with every step the Grullo took.

They reached the Colorado river at Columbus and crossed on the hand-drawn ferry there. Lanny said, "It's a pity we ain't got the time to sight see. This here's a historical spot—you got your old Indian village they call Montezuma, though I don't know why, and you got your castle some scotsman built forty or fifty years back, though I don't know the why of that, neither. And no tellin' what else."

They left the horses at a stable for a good watering and a feed of oats, found a cafe where they ate a pile of tamales served by a pretty Mexican girl, then rode with purpose, reaching the Bigboy headquarters late in the day.

CHAPTER 8

The main house was built of pine logs, "Hauled down from Bastrop," Lanny said, separated into two sides by a dog trot in the middle, fenced by cedar pickets, the yard around it hardpacked dirt. The foreman, Rudy Sterns, lived in one side of it with his wife; the other was kept in reserve for visits by the owner. Out back of the house were the pens and buildings that made handling livestock possible, a barn built of dark red stone and a bunkhouse for the ranch hands of the same dense, heavy stone. Over everything was the smell of manure and the look of hard use.

They unloaded the horses and turned them into the pasture where a remuda grazed, and hunted up some food at the log kitchen that sat in the same yard as the house. Nobody there, but a pan of biscuits waited on top of the wood stove. Lanny stirred the coals and put on a pot for coffee and located some salt pork that they fried.

Sterns hadn't made it in, but his wife, a plump woman with a slight accent Tom couldn't place, showed up while they ate at the big table in the screened porch built onto the kitchen. Her face looked puffy, like she'd waked up from a siesta.

"Where's Rudy?"

"He said he was gonna look for another hand around Houston," Lanny said through a mouthful of bread and meat. "He'll be on pretty soon, I expect."

"I thought he had the winter covered," she said. She looked sweaty and uncomfortable. The afternoon had turned hot. Hard to believe fall had come and cold weather not far off.

"Well, little Hal Jones found him a girl in New Orleans and ain't coming back, and Pinky has lit out for New Mexico. Missin' his wife, I guess. Rudy hired Tom, here, to ride line with me, and far as I know Francisco is still among us, though I have not talked to him. So I think we're just one man short."

She said to Tom, "Lanny has no manners. I'm Loretta Sterns."

He stood on sore and complaining legs and said, "Tom Cloud. Pleased, ma'am."

"Finish your meal. I would have cooked more, but didn't know when to expect you."

Lanny said, "Rudy's got her enlisted as cook slave til spring."

"Soon as we get you boys spread out won't be nobody but me and Rudy to take care of," she said. "You can be your own cook slave then, as you call it."

"It's a hard life you have chose, Tom. Can you make a biscuit?"

He swallowed coffee. "I've been known to. I doubt we'll starve."

Loretta Sterns said, "Any left?" She headed into the kitchen.

Lanny said, "We saved you some. And there's fresh coffee, too."

When he walked out of the bunkhouse in the morning, his legs still as sore as if he'd taken a beating, a buckboard was parked up by the house. He figured the foreman had made it in during the night. Tarver had already dressed and disappeared. Smoke from the kitchen was a pleasant stain in the cold air he breathed, and the wind was out of the north with clouds riding it.

Lanny and Sterns were already into eggs and steak. He got some coffee and sat down.

Sterns said to Lanny, "Take today to ride this man around, break him in a little, show him the remuda and let him pick out one to take with you."

Tom said, "I got a horse already."

Lanny said, "You'll need two, take turns on 'em so they can rest every other day."

"Oh. Well, that makes sense." He spoke to Sterns. "Thanks for the job if I forgot to say that before. Did you find another man?"

"Yeah. He'll be on in a day or two. I think we're set."

An hour later Tom was suffering in his new saddle. "How long am I gonna hurt this way?"

The little man laughed like it was funny. "I don't know. I been on a horse my whole life. But I know what you're talking about. I've seen grown men nearly cry from it. Grit your teeth and stay with it's all I can tell you. You'll get used to it."

A Mexican they called Francisco showed up at the bunkhouse that night, a slight man in pants so tight it looked like he'd been born in them. He had little to say, and the next day Tom asked Lanny about the man.

"It ain't that he don't like us. He just don't talk much. Whoever's the new hand Rudy hired better bring him a deck of cards for solitaire, because he won't have conversation to keep him company."

"Did Loretta stay here by herself the whole time you were on the drive to New Orleans? How'd she take care of everything?"

"I expect she could, but no, a couple of men stayed here most of the time. The busy time is spring roundup and all the brandin' and such, and later on is the drive to market. Drovers come and go on all these ranches. Most work from spring through the drive and take the winter off. The only work then is what me and you is about to do. Rudy keeps a few men on for line riding, but not much else goes on in the cold weather."

Tom worked his new lariat every day, stretched it between his saddle horn and a snubbing post in the middle of one of the pens, faced the pony toward the post and set him back against it like it was a steer he'd roped. The grullo turned out to have good sense—more than Tom, it seemed to him, when it came to cows. Lanny's horse was a cutter, would go into a herd and once Lanny picked an animal would cut it out of the bunch. And keep it out.

The rope lost its stiffness at about the same rate Tom's legs lost theirs, and finally he tried it on a longhorn steer, felt a thrill he hadn't imagined when the loop settled over the wide horns, but neither had he imagined how fast the grullo would brace against the weight. For a second Tom thought his feet would pop right through the stirrups, but the heels of his boots kept his feet where they belonged. Under his breath, as the steer hit the end of it and fell, the grullo backing up and keeping the rope taut, he said to himself, "Thanks, Lanny."

CHAPTER 9

The line shack was barely big enough to sleep two men, made of boards turned gray with time and weather under a rusty tin roof. It held a coal-oil lamp, a pot-belly stove, two bunks and three straight chairs, and smelled like mold and dust from disuse. They stacked their provisions in a corner, enough to get by for a few weeks, boiled a pot of coffee and pulled two chairs outside into the fresh air. The four horses grazed hobbled on some tall Johnson Grass a hundred yards away. Beside the shack a spring of cold water spread itself. Somebody had long ago dug it deeper and ringed it with rocks, the rocks now a part of the landscape with grass grown between and around them so that it all looked natural, like man had no hand in its making. There were brown oak leaves in the bottom of the little pool and the water gave off a good scent that anyone who ever drank from a spring would recognize.

It made good coffee. Tom sipped from his cup and his mind gave him a picture he hadn't seen for a while—O'keefe's eyes turning up the way they did, and he had to blink his own eyes and force them onto the northern hill to escape the vision and the feeling that went with it. Hard to believe he'd been in that alley just a few weeks ago and now sat a thousand miles away watching a hill in the blue distance.

Lanny said, "It's late enough we might as well let the poor old horses alone to graze. You ain't shot that new Colt yet. Maybe it don't work."

"I expect it works fine."

"Well, still I'd like to see you shoot it before I turn you loose by yourself in the morning."

"What's out here that could hurt me?"

"Not much. Let's see...lobos, mountain lions and rattlesnakes come to mind quick. And you got your rustlers to think about. Cow thievin' goes on all the time. Maybe a wild *ladino* bull on the prod, or a few hungry apaches. Let me think a minute..."

"No need. I got your point."

They made a target of an old rusted tin can from the dump out back, set on a stump. Tom loaded five of the new metal cartridges and paced off thirty steps from the can. The revolver felt good in his hand—it had been a while since he'd used one, but his hand remembered, and his arm and eye. He missed the first try, and it deafened him. The Colt had a hard kick, but the trigger pull was good and he put the next one through the can, then pierced it with the third shot where it lay.

He looked at Lanny and caught a smile.

"Look out, rattlers," the rooster said.

He let the Houston pony rest next morning and saddled the dun mare from the Bigboy. And she was trouble soon as he mounted. She put her head between her legs and crow-hopped in a circle. He got a good hold on the saddle horn and rode it out and she was fine the rest of the day, but it was the same any morning he used her. His legs had lost their soreness by now and he felt easy even after riding all day.

For him it was east every morning for half a day, then dinner on whatever he'd brought from camp, then a half day back. He varied the direction sometimes, but it got boring anyhow, not much happening. There was a wormy cow he doctored, some rattlesnakes that he left alone, knowing Lanny wouldn't like it. But what the tough little man didn't know wouldn't hurt him, and there were two of those wild ladino bulls his partner had mentioned, snuffing and pawing ground, looking for a fight and not getting it from him.

Sometimes one or the other brought in a white tail deer and there was fresh venison for a day or two. Tom dropped a four-pointer with his pistol at what he guessed to be fifteen or twenty yards. He began to wish he'd bought a saddle gun when he had the chance.

Days went by like that until the norther rolled in, the first cold weather of the year, blue clouds building and growing all afternoon, then the wind whistling in about midnight, shaking the little shack and making the tin roof rattle. They'd chopped firewood before nightfall, and were quick to build a fire in the stove first thing, the new cold like tiny teeth on their skin. Tom put on his canvas coat and wore it outside to chase down the horses.

They ate beans and biscuits standing up that morning, backed up to the stove. Lanny said, "This cold wind will put the critters on the move. They'll drift south in front of it and you'll find some wanderin' off our range. When you cut a trail go on after 'em soon as you can before they get too far to catch. Just get around in front of 'em and give your pony a free rein. Either one of your mounts is cow smart and will bring the bunch back, with you in the saddle or out of it."

Tom saddled his gelding. He didn't feel like fighting the mare in the cold. He glanced off at the north hill. The wind had died down since daylight and somewhere on the other side of that hill a thin cord of smoke hung in the air. Lanny saw it, too.

CHAPTER 10

"I expect it's either rustlers or Indians. Make sure that thumb buster's loaded."

As he fell in behind the other man Tom felt his heart begin to race and his breath start to come faster, like he'd felt the first time he ever went into battle long years before. And though he breathed faster, it seemed he couldn't get enough air. His face turned hot and his hands cold and trembly and he felt sweat begin to soak into his shirt under his arms. He was afraid and admitted it to himself. Couldn't believe how afraid. The fear was tied some way to a dead man in an alley in St. Louis, Missouri. He had not outrun it after all.

Lanny reined up and said something Cloud couldn't make out. Below them in a motte of scrub oak a man was hitching two mules to a wagon. Two other figures moved around the fire. One wore a dress.

"Just some settlers comin' through," Tarver said. He packed a bolus of snuff under his lip. "Might as well say howdy." They rode down the north side of the hill and Cloud watched the man finish with his mules and walk over to the fire. The woman handed him something, a cup of coffee, probably, and as he drank from the cup his eyes settled on them. He gave her back the cup and went to the wagon, brought up a shotgun and came forward to meet them, leaving the muzzle of the weapon pointed at the ground.

Cloud felt as limp as a slice of raw bacon, relieved that the smoke was caused by neither rustlers nor Indians, nobody requiring a fight. He was ashamed of his fear. How could he live with such as that? What had happened to his courage?

Lanny wrapped his reins around the saddle horn and held up both hands in a good humored show. "No harm, friend, couple of lonesome cowpunchers is all we are."

The man before them was heavy-set, somewhere in his middle years. He was bald-headed, but his mouth hid under a mustache the size of a cottontail rabbit and about the same color. He stared a bit in silence, seemed to decide they were no threat, then smiled and said, "We got some coffee left."

The BB riders slid down and shook the man's hand, Lanny taking the lead and giving their names.

"I'm Florian Weiss, gentlemen." His accent was as heavy as seasoned oak. "There is my daughter Maria and my son Tobias. They don't speak English real good, but like all smart German children, they know their names." As they must have, because the girl gave a quick little bow and the young man nodded. Exhausted as his emotions were, Cloud noticed that the girl was a beauty, dark of eye and hair, a black scarf wrapped over her ears and tied in a pretty bow under her chin.

They took the cups she offered as Florian Weiss said, "We'll be soon out of here, nothing but the wagon tracks behind."

Lanny told him, "You're just fine, sir. It's all open range hereabouts, people is free to come and go, long as they don't rustle our stock. I bet you're headed over to New Braunfels." Cloud couldn't pull his eyes away from the girl's graceful movements. She turned a shy glance at him and quickly looked away as if he'd caught her at something forbidden.

"I have a cousin there, yes, and a few friends, but no. My place is north, past Fort Mason. You know it?"

"I been up there, yeah. Not in a long time, though."

"My farm," the German said. "I didn't leave it." There was something in the man's voice. Anger? Sadness?

Cloud tasted the hot, bitter coffee. "I don't understand," he said, and Lanny's sideways look told him it was a comment he ought not to've made.

"No? Then you are new here, ja?"

"That's right."

The young man named Tobias splashed water on the fire and wet smoke enveloped Cloud for a moment, like a stinking hand wiped across his face.

"I tell you, then. My family come here from Germany before your war. Other families, too. We come for the land, to farm, raise our kids. You know? These two here was this high." He bent over and held the palm of his free hand a couple of feet off the ground. "We have no slaves and we don't like secession, you see?"

"I think so, yessir." There'd been no slaves on the Nashville farm, either. Cloud pulled his bandanna from his hip pocket and wiped at the smoke stink in his nose.

"Some Germans join the army, most of us say no, we would not fight for such a cause, and pretty soon it was *shoot the Germans,* from the other settlers around us. They killed us. They called us Yankee lovers. Can you believe it? Many of us left here, ran away across the Rio Grande to escape. Me? My family I send away to Mexico, my wife and my children. But I stay, I do not leave my farm."

Lanny said, "No offense, Mister Weiss, but why don't you just let it lay? That's all in the past and better left alone."

The large man went over to the wagon and put the shotgun away, picked up his cup where his daughter had left it and said, "I send them away to save their lives, and only now, when their mother has died, do I bring them back to Texas where there is still hatred of us." He shook his head. "The past? No past is big enough to hold all the bad things I saw. And may see again. May see again."

As they rode away from the camp Tom said, "What was that about? That stuff he said?"

"Was a feud got started, like you heard. I was off somewhere else most of the war, but there was killin' all right. It was a bad time, and he was right. It ain't over yet." He reined his horse another direction and trotted off.

For days afterward, the pretty girl's face stayed with Cloud, always coming to mind at night as he waited to fall asleep, then

33

he began to forget as the days piled up, colder and wetter, and many cattle drifted into the southern range in front of the winter winds. Rudy Sterns was the only other face they saw through most of the season, the only other voice they heard. Sterns brought provisions every couple of weeks, hauling them in a two-horse buggy. And at Christmas a pint of whiskey. A few ice storms hit the country that year, but the water stayed open and the cattle grazed the dry grass.

Every day was hard. The horses and men grew leaner with effort. The cold began to ease. Tom could hardly remember the life he'd left, felt at home with the work, the animals, the country he'd come to.

One night as they watched the dance of shadows from the coal-oil lamp, Lanny Tarver came out of his own silent thoughts and said, "We're nearly done here. Won't be long til the cow crowd comes in for the spring work."

Trouble came first.

CHAPTER 11

Cloud was riding the dun mare, headed home and thinking about supper when he saw the smoke. Couldn't miss it. The sun was nearly down and the column of smoke took on the glow of it, hanging there like a golden thread, feathered at the top by wind. A pretty sight, like the blossom he'd seen earlier on a tree he couldn't name.

The mare didn't like it when he reined her that direction. She was thinking about supper, too, he guessed. Rudy had brought out some feed corn and oats for the horses when that first icy spell hit, and every trip since.

He was full of questions, not sure what he ought to do, but figured Lanny had seen the smoke, too, and would be heading that way. Maybe they'd run into each other. Probably more settlers coming across the range, but he checked his revolver, made sure it was loaded, and felt heat in his face and a fine tremor in his fingers. He pushed on.

A stand of mesquite trees was in his way and he rode around it to avoid the thorns, came to the western side of the clear pasture he figured the smoke was rising from, and the mare nickered. His partner was there waiting.

"Travelers?" Tom said.

Lanny looked mournful. He shook his head. "No, I done looked. It's a branding fire. Three men. Nobody from the Bigboy, I can tell you that." He smiled, but it was a mournful smile. "I was hoping you'd show, to back me up."

"What do we do?" His throat was so tight he had trouble talking, felt his heartbeat like a hard punch in his chest.

"Well, early as it is, it could still be some neighbor brandin' his own calves. All I know to do is ride in and ask."

"All right."

"Gun loaded?"

Cloud nodded.

Lanny pulled his Winchester out of its sheath and laid it across the pommel of his saddle. "Let's go." He took the lead.

The men had just finished putting a brand on a new calf and had turned it loose. It ran bawling toward a longhorn cow at the edge of the big clearing. The three men saw them early on and watched as they approached, nobody moving for a weapon.

Lanny said, "Howdy, folks. What's your business here?"

One of the strangers said, "Never mind us, what's yours?"

"I work for Billy Barnett, friend."

"Us, too."

Tarver took a while to respond to that. He brought the rifle around and said, "No, you don't." Cloud had not seen the man in back, shielded by the other two, draw a gun, but it was in the hand he raised, and he used it to shoot Lanny Tarver out of his saddle. Even as Tom reached in reflex for his own pistol he felt sick fear in his belly. The crazy dun mare reared at the sound of the shot that dropped Lanny and began her stiff-legged hop. Tom grabbed at the saddle and hung on as a bullet clipped the sleeve of his shirt, knew if he fell off the rustlers would shoot him, too.

Everything was happening so fast he couldn't think, couldn't react except to feel disgust with himself, shame at his terror. His ears rang from the loud pistol shot. He spurred the mare and she broke into a run. He laid his body against the saddle horn and rode through the mesquites, not feeling the thorns that tore off his hat and most of his shirt and left him bleeding from a dozen cuts.

The strangers circled around the mesquites and that gave him half a minute of lead time. The mare was tired, but so were those other horses, and he knew the country from riding it for months. One good thing about the fear—it made him reckless, and he pushed his mount through narrow spaces and down steep banks that were better avoided. He pulled the mare to a hard stop and listened. The ringing in his ears was gone. He could hear again, but there was no sound of the men or their horses. Newborn coward that he was, he still had to make himself go back and see anyway. Lanny might still be alive.

A shout filtered to him through the heavy timber, from a long way off. Had they lost track of him? Maybe so. He dismounted and knelt on the ground holding the reins in one hand, the .45 in the other, willed himself to calm down, waited like that until good dark, limp and sleepy after the fear burned itself out, and then rode slowly out of the trees in starts and stops, gun high, eyes and ears tuned to every sound.

He knew he was close to the clearing when he felt the mesquite thorns again and saw his hat waiting like a gray memory on the dark ground. He guided the mare around to the other side, then walked her slowly into the open. Cold wind and a half moon out there, a small blaze off the coals of the branding fire. Hard to make things out, but a shadow lay on the ground and when he dismounted and looked close he found the cowboy where he had fallen, arms reaching as though he'd tried to pull himself out of danger.

Cloud touched Lanny's face, turned him over and felt for a heartbeat. No movement, no life. He smelled the sweet, metallic scent of blood, felt it slick and sticky under his shaking hand. He had done the same for many a fallen man in years past, but this one caught at his breath. Fear had run it's way through him like a flooded river and left him washed out and weary. He waited for the strength to stand up, nothing in him but despair and grief, and just then heard a whispered intake of breath.

"Lanny?" He felt his own heart run. "Lanny? It's Tom. You hear me?"

Another breath, stronger this time, a slight movement and a voice so soft it might have been imagined. "I believe they've killed me."

CHAPTER 12

He'd seen a gray Percheron work horse in the Bigboy remuda the fall past when he'd roped out the dun mare. The animal was high as his own head, with hoofs the size of dinner plates. Today he saw that big horse again out in front of the riders coming to meet him halfway back to headquarters. The man riding it had to be Billy Barnett.

Four of them—Barnett and Sterns, and two young strangers. The owner was not quite the giant Lanny had described, but he was big enough, towering a foot over Cloud when they dismounted. His voice sounded like it came from the bottom of a barrel.

"We heard there was rustlers in the neighborhood. Decided to come check on you boys. Where's Tarver?"

He told them the story. "He was alive in his bunk when I left, but I couldn't tell how bad he's hurt and was afraid to put him on the horse."

Rudy Sterns said, "What about the other crew? Francisco and the new man?"

"I don't know. I started this way looking to get help soon as I got Lanny settled."

Barnett said, "You look wore out. Go to the house and get you something to eat. We'll ride on and see about things."

He felt a great relief at that. This new man he'd become, this man who behaved in shameful ways, rode the crazy mare to the horse pasture and turned her loose and left his rigging on the ground outside the gate.

Loretta Sterns had a pot of stew cooking, but not done yet, so she fried some eggs and beef and fed him that along with biscuits left from morning. Cloud didn't feel hungry, but knew he had to eat. The worst of it was he could see by the look on her face she wanted to talk about it. She cleaned the dishes off the table and then she came back and sat down beside him.

"Things go on," she said. "Men coming in for the roundup now, be new calves to brand, a new herd of steers off to market. Things go on. That Lanny, he is a good man, you know?"

"I'm leaving." It was a strange thing to come out of his mouth, because he had not known he was about to say it. She didn't seem surprised.

"Stay and help with the spring work. These feelings will pass."

"I'd like to go right now."

"We have to wait for Rudy if it's what you want to do, so he can pay your wages."

"Couldn't you pay me?"

"You wait for Rudy. He'll be back." She stood up and walked back in the kitchen, leaving him alone with cold coffee.

The others weren't back that evening. He walked out to the horse pasture and brought his rigging in, ate a quick supper with two men he hadn't met before and retreated to the bunkhouse before they could catch him up in conversation. Loretta hadn't said much to him or about him other than a brief exchange of names when she set out the stew. He shucked his boots and crawled under a blanket, knowing sleep wouldn't come, but he avoided inquiries when they came in later with talk and cigarette smoke and the sound of their boots on the wooden floor. He may have dozed—another pair of boots walked across the floor sometime in the night, a bed squeaked when someone lay down on it, but nobody talked, nobody asked anything from him.

Sterns found him before breakfast while he was pulling on his boots. "Billy went up to Bastrop to bring a doctor, left a man with Lanny. Loretta says you want to draw your wages."

"Yes, sir. I'd like to move on."

"Francisco and Barnes is all right."

"Sir?"

"I said Francisco and Barnes is all right. You didn't ask, but I thought you might want to know."

"Oh, yeah. That's good." Cloud felt like he was off somewhere else watching himself talk.

"Lanny always said good things about you. I'd like to keep you on."

He wanted nothing more in the world than to get finished here and leave. "I can't."

"Well, maybe I can understand. Whatever happened out there, nobody blames you for it, you know."

He couldn't reply, didn't want to reply to that. "One thing, they stole my horse. Could I take part of my pay in that mare I been riding?"

"Everybody here hates that horse. You're welcome to her."

Cloud walked alone to the pasture and roped her out, led her to the barn and saddled her. She did her crow-hop while he held on and waited it out, then walked her past the house thinking he ought to wave goodbye. Sterns and his wife sat in chairs on the dog run. Sterns called to him and the two came over to the fence.

"Hate to lose you, son. But good luck to you."

Cloud thanked him.

"We think we know them men you got crossways with. Couple of brothers name of Crenshaw got a little place west of here. They been known to use the running iron, but never been known for shootin' people before."

"There was a third one."

Sterns shrugged. "Hired man, maybe. I don't know. The law's still pretty thin out here, but there's a militia, and I'll be talking to them. Don't reckon there's anywhere we can reach you at in case they want to hear it from you."

"No, sir. I don't...there's no place."

"Go on, then. Take care of yourself."

CHAPTER 13

Cloud headed north and forded the Colorado River, then followed it along its western bank. He had no purpose in mind except to put distance between himself and the Bigboy. Nobody blamed him, Sterns had said, but that made no difference. He knew the truth.

The river led him past Austin into the Hill Country. Rocky ground, clear water and cold nights, no company but the horse he rode and the pipe he'd bought at a little store under a tall oak beside the Pedernales river. He liked the pipe mainly because it reminded him of his father's pipe, the stem curved down and up so it fit his hand when he held it.

He came on stone fences, some as high as his head, dry-stacked limestone settlers had used to fence off pastures, rode around them and went on deeper into the hills with their live oaks and cedars, their whitetail deer and mesquite thorns, their rattlers and spiny cactus. Lost track of time.

It might have been a week or a month since he'd come into the uplift. Cloud crested a hill and instead of another hill, this time a valley swung down before him, all green with grass and misty blue with morning fog and distance, and tucked away in a corner of it, rooftops. The sight of it answered some need in him, caused a quickening of his senses. He climbed down and found a boulder to sit on, lit the pipe and gave himself a few minutes to think it through. He burned the tobacco down, emptied the ashes out of the pipe and climbed back in the saddle. The mare must have been tired, offered him no resistance. He rode downhill.

"I can use you, all right," the foreman said. "We've got the spring work in front of us. The thing is, and I don't know if you noticed it, while we run a good herd of cows, we run some sheep, too. Most of the cowhands I talk to won't mess with 'em. They're a lot of work, and they're dumb beasts."

"That's okay by me." The man standing in front of Tom Cloud carried excess weight on his body, a red-faced man with a friendly air about him.

"There's four men and myself, and a crew comes through every spring, Mexicans, does the shearing. With the sheep, what we do is pen 'em and we dock the lambs and cut the young bucks. Good market in the north for meat now. Nobody down here eats it."

"Yessir, I've handled sheep. My father keeps some on his farm."

"Back in Tennessee, you said?"

"Close to the Smokies." Cloud realized then what had stopped him on sight of this valley. It had a familiar look about it.

"So, like I said, I can use you, but there's one more thing." The man looked embarrassed. "Last couple of years Miz Schneider—that's who owns the place—she has to talk to anybody I hire."

"Well, I don't mind that."

"Come on, then, and I'll take you up to the house."

The red-faced man, whose name was Ward Dobbins, led the way around a rail fence and Cloud followed him onto a gallery that stretched across the front of the house built of boards and batts, unpainted lumber long ago boiled gray by the sun. The gallery held two rocking chairs with tall backs. A tangle of honeysuckle on a wooden trellis screened the southern end of it.

She was gray-haired and compact, a woman of age well-tended, her face without the wrinkled look he saw on most of the women-folk he'd encountered. Dobbins introduced them and spoke a few words then left them alone, closing the door behind him. She did not offer Cloud a seat in one of her parlor chairs, but kept him standing.

"So," she said, "I have only one question for you." Her eyes were bright blue and seemed to take him in from head to toe.

44

Here was the German accent that kept popping up in this hill country. "Will you fight?"

The last thing he'd expected. He was unable to answer her. He felt a strong pulse in his throat.

"You hesitate, I see. Many do. Let me show you something." She opened the front door and crooked a finger at him, then led him across the gallery to the honeysuckle, his boots echoing on the rough boards. Something dark had soaked into the wood where she stopped. He willed his heart to slow down, but it raced on.

"I never washed it off. My husband died here years ago. While you were off at war, I imagine. Somebody shot him with one of the buffalo guns from far away. Look here." She pointed to a board's splintered edge. "Through him the ball went and made that. Whoever it was that shot, I know who sent him— that man out there that thinks the world belongs to him only." She motioned with her chin somewhere southwest.

"So, my question, because they shoot at us even to this day. They threaten us while we try to do our work."

"Why?"

Her mouth turned down, she shrugged. "We didn't like secession. We came here from Germany." The same words Cloud had heard from someone else not so long before. "We raise sheep now, and they don't like that. Some of your Americans don't know it's a free country. They shoot at us, we shoot back. Will you fight? I won't hire you otherwise."

His heartbeat had slowed, felt like it had stopped altogether. A feeling of sadness came over him like a dark night. He shook his head.

"Sorry, ma'am."

"Don't be sorry. It is my fight, not yours. Goodbye, then. Good luck to you." She left him standing there, went inside the house and shut the door. He put his hat back on his head and went to find the crazy dun.

CHAPTER 14

He camped beside a clear creek that night, as far as he could ride from the ranch house with the blood-stained gallery. The coffee he boiled, the tobacco smoke from his curly pipe, were no comfort. A cold rain woke him in the night, hissing on the coals of his fire. He put his slicker on and found the hobbled mare, brought her close in and tied her to a sapling. There was thunder in the distance, and he knew it wouldn't take much to send her on some wild leg-breaking run, leaving him afoot in a strange land.

The lightning and thunder kept him awake the rest of the night and the cold rain left him aching and tired. He rebuilt the fire. He had no desire to travel on; staked the mare in tall grass near the creek and let the morning pass. When you had nowhere to go, could go anyplace you chose, choice became harder, became impossible at times, and all that freedom became no freedom at all.

San Antonio was somewhere to the south, he guessed, not sure of his whereabouts. Maybe he'd go there, find work in the town that didn't require anything of him. Everybody knew about the Alamo, the men who'd died there, many of them his fellow Tennesseans. Brave men. Not like him. Maybe he shouldn't go there after all.

In the early afternoon he doused the fire and saddled the dun. She didn't offer to pitch. The night had left her tired, too. For want of direction he just followed along the creek in a general meander. This was wild country. He saw only one other sign of settlement, a cabin built of cedar logs not far from the creek, enclosed by one of those stone fences. Between the old cabin and the creek a good-sized pen still stood, made of slender cedar pickets driven into the ground side-by-side, with strips of what appeared to be rawhide woven into the pickets and holding the pen together. It hadn't been used for a long time. Tall grass and two mesquite trees grew inside it and some of the rawhide had rotted. But it still looked in pretty good condition. The cabin, on the other hand, had suffered a collapsed roof. Its walls were charred inside. Nobody had lived there for many years. For half a mile above and below the cabin the creek was lined with pecan trees, trees like he'd seen nowhere else, some of them three or four feet thick through the trunks, tall enough to throw a deep shade. Squirrels barked everywhere. They hadn't made off with all the pecans, though. He collected a hatfull and cracked them as he rode, eating the sweet meat and watching the day approach sundown.

"Hey! Hold up there!"

Cloud halted the mare, felt the now familiar pounding of sudden fear, and located two riders coming at a lope. Nothing he could do but wait. They had rifles out. He thought of the silver dollars in his saddlebag, wages from the Bigboy, along with the money still left from his St. Louis winnings. His peacemaker was in there, too. Too late to reach for it.

The lead rider was a heavy man, his face brown as the saddle he sat in, mouth turned down in permanent dissatisfaction. The rider pointed his rifle at Cloud. "Get off that horse." Cloud did as he was told, thinking of death and not minding it. A better destination than San Antonio, maybe.

The two riflemen lit and the heavy one said, "I've warned you people to stay off my range."

Cloud's voice came out thinner than he liked. "I don't know what you're talking about."

"That Dutchwoman knows to keep away from me. Same goes for any of you works for her." This might be the man she had mentioned. Somebody she feared. His face heated up, his lips stiffened.

"No, sir, I don't work for nobody. I'm just passing through."

The second rider was a head shorter than his partner, younger and stronger looking. He came a couple of steps closer and slammed the barrel of his rifle against Cloud's head, knocking his hat a dozen paces away and putting him on his knees. His face was numb and he tasted blood. The stranger said, "You're a liar."

Tom remembered watching a poleaxed steer go down and felt much the same. He shook his head in some kind of dumb, surprised denial.

"We ought to hang him."

"No, son. I want to send him back with another message. Put your gun down and hold him."

The son held his arms behind his back and lifted him to his feet. The father slammed his rifle butt into Cloud's unprotected belly deep enough to drive out any hope of ever breathing again. He fell, his mouth gaping for air. A sharp boot bit into his back, another one the side of his head. The pain blended with the spasm down the front of his torso, his silent cry for breath. More blows connected. A bone broke—he thought it was his left arm, thought he was lying on his right side but wasn't sure. There was cold water in his face. So much pain it no longer mattered. He was past it and gone someplace else. He opened his eyes.

The father stood over him holding his canteen. "I want you awake."

There was a fire. "Ain't got no iron with us, so I'll make do with your big old knife." Tom lay on the ground, could see almost nothing, rolled his eyes down to look at his arm, saw it turned in a way that said it was broken, saw he had no pants on. A leather string was wrapped around his ankles.

"Get his left hip up here now, Phil." He laid the knife on the small fire and left it there, turned back to Tom. "I put my brand on the left hip." Minutes passed in silence as the knife heated. Tom tasted blood, smelled thick smoke, and waited for what he knew would be more pain, knew he had only half his senses about him and was glad of it, wished he could be unconscious or dead.

The big man brought the cherry-red blade to Tom's hip and with it traced something on his skin.

He must have passed out, but it couldn't have been for long. The two men were still there. They'd rolled smokes and stood like shadows against the darkening colors of the sky. They saw that he'd come around.

"Here's your message. You get back to that old Dutchwoman, you tell her I'll hang the next one comes around me. You hear? My stock waters on that stream and I'll have no interference from any of you." Tom managed to nod his head, felt his right ear scrape the ground with the movement, felt a sharp crease of pain in his neck.

The younger man took the dun's reins, said to his father, "I want to try out this mare. Might as well take her home with us." He swung into the saddle and just as quick she bucked him off. He hit hard and came up drawing his pistol. Without pause he shot her between the eyes and watched her fall.

The two men mounted up and rode away without so much as a look back. He could hear them laughing.

CHAPTER 15

He smelled a wet dog. It was licking at his face. He opened his eyes and yelled "Get away!" What started out as a yell ended up being a whisper, but the dark shape moved back anyway. A coyote. He remembered what had happened, who he was, what he had to do if he wanted to go on living, wasn't sure if he did, then thought about it a while and became very certain that he did. He rode the certainty like it was a horse running under him and lifting him off the cold ground.

They had broken him good, like he'd never been. He didn't know if he could move, but tried it, and if he ignored the hurt for a second or two at a time he could use his right arm, which was not ruined like the other one, and raised himself up to a sitting position that left him so dizzy he nearly fell back over. He fought the dizzyness until it slowed down and after that he was still sitting.

The pigging string was around his ankles and it took him a long time to get it loose. All the while he felt like he was freezing in the damp night. If he could stand up and walk, maybe he could find his pants and boots. Still had the shirt on, at least. He stuffed the pigging string in a front pocket, knowing he wanted to keep it without knowing just why. Tiny steps were necessary. Anything else caused a crank in his back that was on the edge of being more than he could bear.

The coyote had retreated from him and gone out of sight, probably getting a bite off the crazy mare. It wasn't that he'd liked her much, but the thought of a stranger killing her like that put fire in him.

He found the jeans, stiff and cold in the grass, but he couldn't raise a leg high enough to get them on, and every time he tried it, a new pain cut at his hip, the left one, and his searching right hand had a hard time reaching around to touch the wounded place, feel of it, understand what had been done. Starlight reflected off the knife that lay in short grass and he heard the words again—*I put my brand on the left hip.*

He was thirsty, felt so dry the wind might blow him away. The empty canteen rested a few paces from his knife. Where was the creek from here? Must be close; hadn't he been riding along its banks when they stopped him?

Water was what he needed. Once he realized it he could think of nothing else and took tiny barefoot steps in search of it, coming down on some kind of small button cactus that put a thorn in his foot and left it there, and he went on because it didn't matter when he needed water so much, and its pain was just one more hurt.

Not far ahead he heard it. Some twist in the slow current of the creek sent off liquid slaps, sounding to him like encouraging words from a friend. He feared not being able to rise again, so only knelt beside it in wet grass and filled the canteen from it. He drank it dry and filled it again, knowing he had to wait a little bit to drink more, yet drinking more anyway because he couldn't stop. His stomach cramped and he threw up most of the water. The spasm passed. He sipped again from the canteen and kept it down this time.

A tree—one of the big pecans—loomed close and he got himself upright again and went to it, leaning against the rough bark, smelling the creek and the wet rocks it ran on, the perfume of greening leaves. He went down on aching knees and waited through the thick night for dawn.

Morning gained him nothing.

The aches had doubled their torment and he shook with chills. His face was hot, and not from fear. Fever had set in. He drank from the canteen again and hobbled to where the dead mare lay, managed to get his bedroll untied and dragged it back to the tree. It was lucky he still had it. If they'd ridden off with her then his pistol, his wages, this blanket and slicker, would be gone as well.

His good arm worked well enough to get the blanket around him and he spread the slicker beside the tree, lowered himself into a sitting position and leaned back against the pecan, his head swimming with the fever. His pants were next to him, but his boots were still out there in the grass with everything else. Wings thumped the air and two black buzzards settled next to the mare's belly and began to tear at her. He couldn't keep his eyes open. He fell off steeply into sleep and dreamed he was in his mother's arms.

She touched his face and said something he couldn't understand, moved the broken arm and caused him such pain he opened his eyes. Her face was there, but she had changed, not the woman he remembered. Was this a dream? Another face behind her and another. Her hand gave him water, bitter water, but he swallowed it, and a child's voice said, "You sleep. You get well." It could have been his brother who spoke, but hadn't he died in a war? It was hard to remember, and Cloud was very cold.

CHAPTER 16

He thought a bee had gotten into his head and was buzzing around trying to get out. That's how it felt, anyhow. Not a real sound, just a feeling, and he moved his head to make the feeling stop.

A place he'd never seen was drying up in his thoughts like dew under a morning sun. It was a place of strange light and emptiness, and a rainbow of colors. He didn't want to let it go. It left him, anyway, dried up and vanished from his thoughts and he slept again, this time without dreaming, unfevered and healing.

"Wake up now. You eat." He smelled charcoal, the residue of burned wood, opened his eyes inside the ruined cabin he'd come past long before. Above him was a makeshift cover of green branches, their leaves his sky. A child stood near him, a girl. She said, "Good. You eat." A bowl was in her hand. She put it to his lips and he swallowed thin corn mush. He couldn't believe how good it tasted.

The girl was probably ten years old, a Mexican child with black eyes and braided hair and high Indian cheekbones. He wanted to ask her questions, but then was too tired to form words and let himself slide back to sleep.

She stood there again when he woke and he realized that she had said something or had shaken his shoulder. This time was better. She fed him from the bowl again, and the plain food tasted good again. He swallowed the last of it and heard himself ask, "What happened?"

It must have been night time, almost everything dark around him, but the girl carried a burning stick that offered up a small flame. Smoke stung his nose and made him twist his head away, causing the crease of pain in his neck. The men, the beating, tore into his mind like a hard fist. His arm. He bent his neck and looked at the binding around his chest that kept the arm in place. Looked for his naked legs and saw them covered by his pants. Somebody had dressed him. On his right wrist, wrapped around it like a bracelet, three dulled colors. Red, yellow, black. The rainbow.

"Who are you?"

She didn't reply, left the ruined cabin with her lighted stick. He heard voices from outside. More than one male, a woman or two, the girl. It was her he'd thought was his brother speaking, himself a child. She came in again, followed by an old woman carrying a coal oil lantern. Flame from the lantern glowed across the woman's face, showing up the dark wrinkles deep in the skin, the gray hair that hung around her head like long, uncombed moss. She spoke to the girl in Spanish.

"Mi abuela say don't be scared."

Funny thing to say. And he was not. Not scared.

"Mi abuela say the eyes gone now."

O'Keefe? He remembered the man, remembered his own sorrow but couldn't bring up the picture of those rolled-up eyes that had been his haunt for so long. How could she know? Maybe he was still in a dream.

"Mi abuela say there is no fault."

"What does she mean?" The tight binding around his chest pushed his speech high up in his throat.

The girl shrugged, stretched her mouth in the manner of all kids and it made him want to smile. She raised a shoulder and repeated, "No fault."

He shook his head, feeling the hurt in his neck. "There is much fault."

"No!" The Mexican child held up a finger as if in warning. "Mi abuela say is NO fault."

"All right." He didn't feel like arguing about something they were only guessing at. He held up his wrist. "What is this?"

The grandmother talked for a long time. He felt himself burrowing into sleep when the girl spoke again.

"Mi abuela, when she young like me, younger than me, pick up a little snake with pretty colors and it bite her on the finger. Somebody kill the snake with a stick, then she can't breathe and she die. Then when she die she go some far place and the snake is there and he say to her go back and heal sick people and my skin your medicine. It is that skin on your arm she use to make you well."

The old woman watched him in the lantern light, gauging his belief. Cloud suspected he would now be a dead man if these people hadn't come along and cared for him. If it was some heathenish myth he was cured by, the magic skin of a snake, so be it. He would not argue it.

"Tell your grandma she has saved my life, and I am grateful."

There was a smile from the girl, a frown from the old woman and they took the light away, leaving him in solid night, but a night that was not so dark as before.

They had come up from somewhere to the south to gather pecans as they did each year; a family of them—the girl and her parents, the grandmother and a grown brother. He never asked their names and they never told him, seemed secretive and quiet when he described the men who'd hurt him. The burn on his hip was a crude circle, drawn with the hot tip of his knife. "Lazo," the grandmother called it.

The girl told him, "Here they say *loop*. Loop brand. Is lasso, too. It is Mister Loup, his ranch. It don't spell the same, but I don't know why."

"Where did you learn English?" None of the others spoke it. Not to him, anyway.

"The mission school."

"You're a fine girl." His praise embarrassed and pleased her. She blushed and ran away.

They had finished with their pecan gathering and were waiting for him before they left—for him to be well, able to feed himself. They were very kind and sang songs in Spanish at night for him, the two men, with a scratched guitar the paint had peeled off of. The women cooked squirrels knocked out of the pecan trees with a single-shot rifle by the brother. They cut the squirrels up and rolled them in corn meal and fried them, and they cracked pecans and laid the nuts on a heavy ceramic plate for him beside the fried squirrel and boiled beans and tortillas. He drank their hot coffee with his food, or sometimes cold water from the creek and got better.

His saddle was there. The good family had stripped everything off the horse and brought it to the burned-out cabin because the fever in him had been high and he needed out of the morning dew, under a roof, even a collapsed one. All his wages were in the saddle bag, the silver dollars Sterns had paid him, and the greenbacks left from his winnings. He tried to give a handful of the silver to them and they wouldn't take it, so he went to each of them alone and asked again. Still, no one would let him do it, though he needed to give them something, and at last he said to the curandera, "Por favor. Please." When he held the money out to her she turned away.

The girl said, "Mi abuela is not take your money for heal you."

They went away next morning, the girl shy with her goodbyes, the men giving him strong handshakes, the father saying to him in rough English, "Misser Loup bad man. Go from here."

The curandera ignored him, or seemed to, but he knew better. It was hard to watch them leave.

His broken arm he kept now in a cloth sling tied around his neck, his gunbelt cinched on his waist full of shells and the long peacemaker loaded and hanging on his right hip where he could get at it. The family of Mexicans had found an iron pot somewhere around the deserted place and left it with him, and he used it to stew the squirrels and rabbits he killed. The pistol made a lot of noise, noise somebody might hear, but he didn't care. It tore up the meat unless he shot the little animals in the head. They'd made him a present of their last sack of coffee, though he tried to refuse it. They'd left him a sack of ground corn, too, and he made mush with it for his mornings. There was nothing but a slight mound of fresh-dug dirt where the dead horse had been, the death-stink of her covered over. His tin cup and the can he had used for boiling coffee had been mashed flat under the mare's weight when she fell, but he used the knife on them and opened them up enough to serve his purpose, and at night he slept well.

Every day he thought about what had happened—not about the men and what they had done to him, the time for that would come later, but about the things the old woman had said. *There is no fault. The eyes gone now.* How had she known about the eyes? The misery that was in him before? And, truth be told, was in him no longer. He felt free again, and stronger every day.

A week after the Mexicans had gone he built a fire in the early evening and let it burn down to coals, then stripped off his clothes and folded them in a pile under a tree. He knelt beside the snapping coals a long time, the thin rise of smoke pleasant in the cooling air, thinking of the far off place he had gone and the rainbow there, and the things that had happened these few days. Shades of red moved in the coals, white ash falling away or lifting into the air when the south wind touched it. Cloud rubbed his fingers over the sore burn on his hip and then he stretched out on his back and rolled over into the coals so that his hip was in them. He left it there until he smelled his flesh burning and the pain became too great to bear. He rolled back into the grass and passed out.

Later he lay in the creek water until the hurt lessened, then dressed himself by starlight and put on his coat because the night was cold. He would live out his life with a burn scar on his hip, but it was a scar of his own choosing.

CHAPTER 17

Ward Dobbins watched him from a long way off coming closer to the clutch of buildings, the house, the barn, the pens of the ranch. The foreman stood with his hat off scratching in his hair waiting to recognize the face of whoever was coming along the narrow valley trail with a saddle over his shoulder. When Dobbins recognized the younger man, saw the way he walked, the way he held his free arm slung against his chest, he came trotting out to meet him and took the saddle off him, putting its weight over his own shoulder.

"Never figured to see you again," he said while they walked on.

"I had some trouble."

"Where's your horse?"

"That's why I came here. I need another one, thought maybe I could buy one off you. Or borrow one til I can find a replacement."

"We'll help you out, sure. Not my business, I guess, but it ain't hard to see you need more than a horse. You've lost some weight and you look mighty tired. It'll be dark in two or three hours. Why don't you sleep in a warm bunk tonight and eat a good feed. You can go on tomorrow."

"Yes, sir. I would...I would welcome that kindness."

The bunkhouse was full, new men hired on for spring work, but they found a folding cot for him and it looked to him to be a luxury after so many nights on the ground. After supper Dobbs told him the woman had asked him up to the house.

This time she did invite him to sit down. He felt out of place in the soft chair, in the clean house with pictures on the wall, a man used to sticks and stones now, burnings and broken bones. She brought him a cup of tea in a heavy mug and put it down on a table beside the chair, sat down herself and said, "You had a hard time out there."

He nodded. "Yes."

"I am thinking you run into my friend, Mister Loup, huh?"

"That's the man. Had his boy with him. Thought I worked for you."

"And did you bring me a message? This has happened already, you see. It's how he talks to me. Lucky for you he didn't do worse."

He told her a little of what happened, left out most of it, drinking from the tea mug now and then. The taste of the tea put him in mind of the war camps he'd lived in that sometimes brewed it strong like this on cold mornings.

"I know that place with the pecan trees. Beside a goat pen is a stone with a name on it."

"A grave, you mean? I didn't see it."

"Yes, a young man who burned down his own cabin and then hanged himself."

"Why would a man do that?"

"He did not, of course. It was the story told by Loup, that's all. Hans Knefler wouldn't fight in the slave war and he wouldn't run away and that wolf killed him."

"I met another German man a while back, by the name of Weiss, I think he said. Farms up here somewhere."

"Yes, I know him. He stayed, like me, and watches his back like me."

Cloud pictured the pretty girl. "Where does he live?"

"North, out on the level land where there is dirt to plow. You go to visit?" She smiled and he had the feeling she knew why he had asked.

"Maybe."

It felt strange to ride into a settled town. Mason had streets and stores and houses where people lived, and a courthouse. He found the County Clerk's office and inquired about a homestead along a creek down in the southern end of the county, never proved out because the owner had died.

62

"Hans Knefler, it says here." The man had found it in a thick ledger. "Already surveyed. No reason you can't pay the back taxes and take it over, prove it out for yourself if that's what you want. A hundred and sixty acres is all it is, though."

"Yes, that's what I want, only I want title to it now. I'll buy it outright."

And when he'd gotten it done and the papers signed he found a store that sold guns.

"I've got a couple of Henrys back here," the clerk told him. "Shoots a .44 rimfire shell. Not very many made, though, and costly little fellers, but a mighty good weapon a man can depend on."

"I need a saddle scabbard to carry it with."

The stable man told him about a horse trader not far from town. The place didn't look promising, but he rode in and asked anyway. The trader turned out to be a female who could've passed for a man if her hair had been shorter. She didn't appear to know what a horse was, exactly.

"A runner, you say?"

"Yes."

"Not a cowhorse?"

He shrugged his shoulders and dismounted. This would take some time. "I'm on a cowhorse now. What I want is a fast one."

She seemed to be thinking it over. "I've got a couple that might fill your needs—one's gelded, the other's hung onto his manhood. Most folks don't want a stallion. They mostly are too hard to handle. You could always do the deed yourself, 'course."

He looked at the Schneider mare he'd bought, a pretty animal, mottled white and black with big, spotted hindquarters. She had appaloosa blood in her. It might be good to raise some colts off her. The woman took him walking back of her stable into a pasture fenced on two sides by stone and the other two by smooth wire on cedar posts. He smelled the sweet scent of hay. A small herd of ten or twelve horses grazed inside it and she pointed to a black one with a thin white blaze down his face. The stallion was tall—stood sixteen hands high with long legs and a clean, well-formed body. He looked like a horse built to run.

"Mind if I get on him?"

When he brought the black up, blowing hard and chomping at the bit in his mouth he dropped the reins into the woman's hand and climbed down.

She said, "What do you think?"

"Leave the saddle on him. I'll need a lead rope for my mare."

CHAPTER 18

The purchase took some haggling, but he came away satisfied. The first colt would pay the money back, and a fast horse might one day save his life. He loaded the mare with the provisions he bought in town, then rode to a saloon. He filled his curly pipe and lit it, got down off the stallion and hitched the reins to the rail out front.

"Bottle of whiskey," he told the bartender.

He pushed back the glass the man put beside the bottle. "No, I'm taking it home with me." Funny thing for him to say. A burned-out cabin wasn't much of a home. True anyway, he supposed.

While he counted out the price one-handed the figure next to him at the bar said, "I sure do like that pipe."

Cloud glanced at him and nodded, finished paying for the bottle and turned to leave.

"Where'd you find that?" The face was whiskey-burnt, eyes set back in the man's head, nose and mouth out in front. For just a second it seemed he'd seen that face before. Reminded Cloud of a razorback hog. And he knew the stranger had no interest in his pipe.

"Store east of here."

A grin. "Well, that's too far to ride for a pipe. Why don't you just give it to me?"

Cloud went on out the door, pleased to note that no thrum of fear had run through him. He put the whiskey bottle in a saddle bag and lifted out the peacemaker, cocked it coming up and had it aimed at the batwing doors when the razorback came through them. The fellow took a second to understand he was anticipated, looked up and down the street like he was checking on the weather and went back in.

He mailed off a letter to Tennessee, this time with better news than that last one he'd posted from New Orleans, then made one last stop at a blacksmith forge on the edge of town. He had the smith check the stallion's shoes for soundness, and told him he wanted a branding iron, and it wouldn't take long to make because the brand he'd just registered was simple as could be.

Everything needed doing at once. First thing, he scouted for the survey stakes at the property corners. They'd drawn him a rough map at the courthouse and he used it to orient himself. The north line of his homestead butted against the Schneider property and the rest of it stuck out in the range claimed by the Loop ranch. The stakes had been broken off at ground level and it took a whole day and part of another to locate the spots and to cut new stakes and drive them into place. The first Loop rider to come along would likely tromp them down again, but he wanted it known he'd come to stay.

A new cabin would have to wait—his arm was not healed all the way, and he'd need both arms to chop logs. He made a leanto shelter out of pecan limbs near the old goat pen and kept the horses inside the pen at night. His weapons were always close and loaded. Sooner or later, visitors would come.

Cloud saw the same possibility in the small holding that Hans Knefler probably had seen—all those pecan trees—fat, brown nuts covering the ground, a crop planted hundreds of years before he was born, yielding up a harvest he had only to gather and get to market. Where the market was he wasn't sure, but knew it was out there, knew good prices were paid. He'd heard talk of a railroad From New Orleans clear to San Antonio. If the talk was true, that was his answer. Louisiana, Tennessee, the Carolinas, all of them could make their pies with his pecans. Another reason, the main reason he'd bought it was that him owning this piece of ground would be like a rock in Loup's boot. Sooner or later the man would try to shake it out.

The gravestone he'd heard the woman describe was covered over in briers and mean little thorn trees that seemed to fight back when he took the axe to them using his good arm. They reminded him of the boxing matches he'd fought. He thought about it while he cleaned off the site. Missed it some, the boxing matches. It had been his means of respect, and after the war his means of earning money. More than that, he understood now, it had been his gift—something as natural as inhaling air, something he did better than most men, and winning left him feeling...what? Superior? Yes, but not to other men. Superior to whatever life might throw at him.

Like now.

And the old curandera was right—the eyes were gone. It had never been his fault. It was the fault of living, and the punches life could throw.

CHAPTER 19

The visitors who came were not the ones he'd expected. He was fitting a handle into an old rusted mattock he'd found in the briers the day he cleaned off the goat-pen grave. Somebody, probably the one who'd buried the young man, had left it there, and the handle had rotted. When he found it Cloud had cut an oak sapling for a new one, and skinned off the bark and left it to season. It was dried out now, and wouldn't shrink more.

He heard one of his horses whinny and by the time he collected the Henry and got behind the stack of rocks he'd heaped there for just this reason, the first rider appeared, coming through the trees. There were five others. When they spotted his rough camp the bunch stopped for a minute. He could hear conversation, but couldn't make out the words, then two of them came forward while four held back with their saddle guns raised.

The two coming at him were slow and careful, watching out for trouble.

The stack was a little higher than his head and he'd built a rifle port in it so he could stand protected and fire through the opening.

"You men stop right there."

Both horses halted. He heard the snap of metal at a distance. He understood that he might be in a bad spot. Understood it and accepted it, but did not fear it. Bad didn't mean hopeless.

"Who are you?" It came from the first rider, the one who seemed to be their leader, a thin whip of a man on top of a sorrel gelding that looked like it had some run in it.

"Same thing back at you," Cloud said.

"Nothing to fear from us if you ain't out here stealing cattle."

"You see any cattle? You're trespassing on my land, mister. Whatever's here is mine."

"I thought this was abandoned land."

"Was. Not now. Who are you?"

"State Militia. Why don't you come out of there and let's talk."

"I might, when you folks put your weapons away." Cloud kept his sights on the man's head, an easy shot if he wanted to take it, and he would if they made a wrong move. The rider turned in his saddle and called back to the others.

"Put them things down. He sounds honest to me. I'll go talk to him and y'all stay back." He shoved his own rifle into the scabbard under his leg and rode up to the rock stack, got down and waited.

One of the men yelled, "Look out for a trap, Captain."

Cloud edged around the rock into sight. The captain smiled at him and said, "This a trap?"

"Why, no. This is me being pestered by such as you."

When the others rode up Cloud realized one of them was the Loup son, the one named Phil, the one who'd held his arms while the old man plowed into Cloud's gut with the stock of a rifle.

"We told you to get off our property." Philip Loup dropped his left foot out of the stirrup and slid to the ground as he spoke, coming at Cloud with quick steps and throwing a punch the second he was in range. Cloud kept his feet in place, moved his head to the left, causing Loup's fist to miss his face by six inches, then went in behind it and delivered a straight right to the man's stomach. Loup went down hard and struggled to rise. He was reaching for his revolver and having trouble pulling it when two of the strangers grabbed hold of his arms.

The captain took the gun. "We're out to protect citizens, Phil. You must have misunderstood the oath when you joined."

"He's been warned off. We sent him running one time, and won't be another warning."

"Well, I'm here to do the job I signed on for and that don't include rousting this man on land he claims is his."

70

Loup shook his head in silence, then said, "Believe I'll just ride on back home, you don't mind."

The captain unloaded the gun and handed it back empty. "Sorry to hear it, but you're free to quit anytime, like the rest of us."

Loup mounted up and swung his horse around to leave, pointed a finger down at Cloud and said, "This ain't over."

"No, sir, it's not." One of the other men rode away with Loup. Cloud thought he might have seen that man before. Another nearly familiar face he couldn't quite place.

He offered them firewood from his pile and they boiled coffee, slouched in a ragged gathering while their ponies grazed. The captain's name was Grant.

"No relation to Ulysses. It was a great embarrassment to me in the late war." Cloud enjoyed hearing him talk, liked his sense of humor, and hadn't failed to notice the man's courage a few minutes before. "Since Loup seems bent on giving you trouble, Mister Cloud, it might be a good idea for you to show me some kind of proof of ownership. You got any papers?"

Cloud had his deed and receipts from the courthouse in a leather pouch inside one of the saddlebags. When he got them out he realized he ought to get a safe or something to keep them in, protect them. This was no way to preserve important documents.

Grant said, "I congratulate you. This is a fine strip of land, though I don't doubt you'll have some contention over it."

They were ranchers and farmers and store clerks, men called out on occasions of Indian depredation or reports of cattle theft. Two dollars a day their wage when they lived to collect it.

Grant said, "I guess it's due to the army leaving Fort Mason. Word got down into Mexico some way and they're not afraid to come up here now." He was talking about the raids on a few settlers in the last month by Lipan Apaches.

One of the others added, "That, and the Comanche is about cleaned out. Comanche is the ones run the Apache bands out of Texas."

71

Cloud said, "Well, I got nothing to steal, I don't imagine they'll bother me."

"That's why we came here," Grant said, with that same smile under his thin mustache. "This here's been Apache country since way back—all up and down this creek, because it's spring fed and runs year around, and because of these very fine pecan trees. Sooner or later they'll swing by for a little banquet. They like horse meat, too, above everything else. Of course, yours are fine looking animals. Hard to say whether that bunch would ride 'em or eat 'em."

"I've got a sack full of flint points I've picked up," Tom said. "I knew Indians had lived here but didn't know what sort."

"That's the sort, all right—Lipans. This was home in the winter to a couple of bands. Rest of the year they moved around, went after buffalo."

"I doubt they'll come around. This Loup fellow would be a tough one for them to go against, and his range is all out in front of me."

"The Loup bunch have not seen hide nor hair of Lipans, but the Indians are not dumb, and I think they're more likely to come on to your place while the ranchmen are busy someplace else with other things. Slip right past 'em."

"How about Schneider? You been there?"

"Next stop."

"Has anybody been killed?"

"Not far as I know, but it's a matter of time. Bound to happen unless we run 'em out. They did hit some people up by the old fort, burned a corncrib and left a man hurt. Man name of Weiss."

From there on, Cloud left off following the conversation, knew talk was going on, but his head filled with memories of a graceful, dark-haired girl and of a winter camp with a wagon hitched up. The four men cooked a meal over the fire and ate it, caught their grazing horses, tightened their cinches and made ready to leave.

He said to Grant, "This Weiss you mentioned is a man I met a while back. He had two others with him, son and daughter. How about them?"

The captain's horse wanted to go, flexed his neck and pranced, his teeth rattling against the bit in his mouth. Grant ignored the animal's agitation. "Unharmed, far as I know. Listen, the militia could use a man like you. Why don't you join up and ride on with us?"

He thought about it. "I might sometime, but there's other things just now."

They were riding off when he thought to ask a question. "The man that left with Loup. What's his name?"

"That's Lynn Crenshaw," one of the militiamen called back. "Him and his brother's thick with the Loups. Got a spread south from here."

CHAPTER 20

It was a bother, but he took both horses. No sense leaving one behind for somebody to steal. He rode the black runner and led his appaloosa mare. Grant had been right about the fort— no soldiers around there anymore. But there were people living inside it; a gathering of frontier types, none of them prosperous looking. He met a white man and an Indian riding side by side on the military road that led past it. The Indian wore a blue coat above a long leather breechclout, and had a wide cloth band around his head. Looked Apache to Cloud, but a tame one if there was such a thing, probably a scout. He pulled the mare to a stop and the other two did the same.

"I'm looking for the Weiss place somewheres around here."

The scout made no effort to answer, but his partner was quick to say, "That the Dutchman got raided?"

"So I heard, yes, sir." The man's beard was so thick Cloud couldn't see his mouth inside it. He had on a fringed buckskin shirt stained dark from use and neglect.

"That stallion looks like he could run. You race him?"

"No. I Just bought him."

"We could get us up a race among all these reprobates at the fort if you a mind to."

"Thanks anyhow, but I want to get on to the Weiss place."

"Too bad. I could use some excitement today." He tipped his hat up on his bald forehead. "Back there two, three miles, leave the road and head north on a wagon trail. You'll run into it."

Cloud guessed at the distance, found a wheel-rutted trace and headed north. He had left the limestone hills behind and come into flat prairie, farmland, good soil a plow could do business in. What he ran into first was a low stone wall not more than three feet tall, just enough to discourage an unmotivated cow. It went out of sight east to west in both directions, ending either way in timber. In front of him, just over the wall, was a crop of some kind. Short stalks with green seedheads. He turned west and followed the track, calculating how much labor must have gone into that fence, how many years expended in hauling and stacking. Where the oaks began it ceased and he rode into the trees and out to the edge of the field and on to the farmhouse. It stood on a sandy hill not far from the remains of the burned corncrib.

The thing that got his attention, though, was the cutting and banging and climbing and hammering going on about twenty paces from the destroyed crib. Six or eight horses switched their tails at flies inside a rail pen. Two buckboards rested at the gate, tongues dropped to the ground, looking like they'd run a hard race and were resting up from it.

Except for the roof a new crib was nearly built. He'd arrived too late to help.

Florian Weiss left the others and walked toward Cloud wiping his hands on a rag. He raised an arm in greeting. "Get down, get down." He didn't look injured or sound it.

Cloud pivoted off the Appaloosa mare and reached out to shake the hand the German offered. "Mister Weiss, I heard you had Indian trouble."

"I have seen you before?"

"Yessir, last fall, you was bringing your boy and girl home."

"That's right, that's right, I remember you now. And the other one, too." Hammers smacked against nails not far away, and men talked loud. The ground was damp from a shower. Cloud could smell the rainy dust at his feet and resin on the hand he had just touched. Weiss's cottontail mustache bounced as he talked. The mention of Lanny was like the quick slice of a sharp knife. Had the little rooster lived or died? He hadn't wanted to think about it or feel the self-guilt again. But soon he'd have to ask the question of somebody, and find out the answer, good or bad. He'd almost told the militiamen about Crenshaw, but without proof what good would it do?

76

He said, "Some militia came by my place and said you got hurt. And burned out."

Weiss laughed. "Ah, me. Rumor and gossip." And while they stood there breathing the fresh air behind the rain shower and hearing the work going on a few paces away, with shortened shadows at their feet from the midday sun, Weiss told him what had happened.

They were only a few, two families and a blind old man who belonged to no one anymore, who came with them because his feet wanted to feel the land of his boyhood again. Sage had allowed it and his wife and daughter had cared for the old man who would anyway die soon. They pulled two tipis of hide and saplings behind horses, for sleeping and for shelter from sun and rain. They had crossed the Rio Bravo twenty days before, planning to travel to Palo Duro Canyon far to the north where the old peach orchards grew. It had been the blind man's home long ago and he talked as he walked, though nobody listened, of the smell that wafted off the blossoms in spring, and of the gold fruit his people had treasured. A few others had come along with fighting on their minds and when they saw that Sage would allow none of it, had gone off on their own looking for trouble.

But it was too far and the land was too settled. They were cut off from the canyon by the changes in the land. He had realized after a few days they could not reach it without fighting, and so began a slow arc back southward.

Only three rode saddle horses, Sage and his son, who was called ish-kay-nay, like all Lipan boys, which simply meant *the boy,* and a man from the second family, Yellow Bow. It was necessary that they rode in order to hunt the game that fed the small band. Their horses were outfitted with Mexican saddles and bridles taken on raids in Mexico years before. They raided no longer, or warred. The Winchesters on the saddles had been used for buffalo many years before, but with those animals wiped out, for deer and pronghorns now. Ish-kay-nay carried a bow and blunt arrows that he used on the rabbits they flushed along the way.

The others, three women and a small boy, took turns on the backs of the two pack horses, balancing in discomfort among the camp essentials lashed there. A people clean by nature, they all smelled of campfire smoke and cedar oil and talked among themselves of the need for rest and washing and the making of a camp.

On that day they had come a very long way. Sage rode in front watching the country ahead. There were whites everywhere, and not many would ask why his band had come here. Sage carried a white cloth in one of his saddlebags, and hoped he would have a chance to wave it in the wind if hostile guns turned their way. Not for surrender. He would never surrender to the white man's will. But for a sign of peace, and his hope for bloodless passage through a land once unscarred by the axe, once a land of buffalo and redmen.

The sun was low behind him, his shadow stretching twenty paces ahead. Dark pockets grew under brush and trees where night was making its nest. Threads of cooler air, thin as buffalo sinew, wrapped around the heat he breathed in. He saw the line of cottonwoods and then the white-silver flash of moving water between the thick leaves. It was the kind of place they needed to find, a wide, flowing creek in the midst of a meadow clothed in tall grass.

While the women unloaded the horses and set up their tipis, Sage and Yellow Bow rode away to look over the country ahead. Reaching the horizon they saw the corner of a stone fence and beyond it the roofs of buildings such as the white men put up.

"That is bad," Yellow Bow said.

"Yes. We will move on." He kept disappointment out of his voice. Somewhere they would come on the right place for the long camp they hungered for and the planting of the seed corn they carried.

"The women are tired."

"There's enough to eat. No need to hunt tonight. We'll be quiet and rest before we leave." No one could have said why Sage was the one who made decisions for everybody, but he always did without objection.

Yellow Bow said, "It will be too late to plant after this."

"It has been too late for a while now. We should have started sooner and left the blind man behind. But we will wait for the change of the seasons and plant another time. The seed is patient."

They smelled boiling meat when they neared the camp again. The flaps of the erected tipis were open, buffalo sleeping robes laid out inside. Sage's wife came to meet him as he slid to the ground.

"The old man is dead," she said.

The weary elder had sat down beside the cooking fire and crossed his legs, sighing in gratitude at the warmth, though the day was hot. And there he'd stayed until someone put a hand on his shoulder and caused him to fall over sideways into the flame, almost knocking over the cooking pot, catching his hair on fire.

"It was over before he fell," said Sage's wife as they stood inside the tipi looking at the body. "He just died sitting there."

Florien Weiss broke off his story long enough to yell to the men around the risen crib. "We have some dinner in a little!" Hands waved back at him to show they'd heard.

To Tom he said, "I come out early that day for the Holstein to get her milked and the dog starts up to barking." He pointed north to the line of trees edging his field. "And there I see two men on horses, one waving a white flag on the end of a stick. They come in slow and I wait and then I see they are Indians, so I go in the house and get my shotgun and I come out again fast because I don't know what they want. Tobias is just get his clothes on and he comes out behind me with his rifle, and the Indians can see we will fight if they come for that."

Sage saw the guns, but they didn't frighten him. He stopped his horse while they were still far enough away from the men to be poor targets in the early light. He waited for a time to see what might happen. Nobody moved, no guns came up to fire. He said to Yellow Bow, "Stay here." He touched a knee to his horse and began a slow walk forward, holding the white flag high, then reined up a hundred paces from the German farmers. In the morning quiet his voice carried the distance between them.

"Friend," he said. It was one of the few words he knew in the language of the white settlers. He lowered the flag and waited again. Soon the big man with the hairy face handed his shotgun to the younger man and then he took a few steps toward sage, his arms out and his hands open showing he carried no weapon.

Closer, he also said, "Friend," and waited.

Sage nodded and slid off his pony. He put the staff on the ground at his feet. Then to the hairy man he said another word some of the whites understood. "Pozole."

CHAPTER 21

"It was what they needed to bury with a man that died, you see? These Indians, they make the hominy from corn, but all they had was seed they saved to plant, and so they come to me. We have a can of it in the kitchen, but they want more, so I make some signs with them and finally we understand that the women will come up here from their camp and do it.

"Me and Tobias get out the iron pot and burn some wood to ashes and two women come with the Indian. He is named Sage, if I got it correct. They boil the water and ashes to make the lye, and we shell some corn. So, about the time the corn is cooked right for hominy a wind comes up and blows a spark on the corn crib."

He pointed to the blackened remains. "That happened."

"And you got burned?"

"A little, yes. My shirt catch fire and burns my back some where you can't see, but Maria dresses it good, and I am okay."

"So the Indians didn't hurt you none."

"No. When the smoke starts they get very scared. The squaw she scoop up the hominy in a sack and they ride away fast."

"You mean they didn't stay to help you put the fire out?"

"No." He shook his head. "But I understand. The smoke brings neighbors. If the people stay maybe folks misunderstand and a fight break out. You see? I think if that Sage feller alone he would stay to help."

A clatter of noise came from back of the house and Tom Cloud looked to see the girl beating a pot with a long stick. "Time to eat," Weiss said. "Unsaddle your horse and put them in that pen over there with the others." Tom turned the mare into the pen, but tied his stallion outside. The black was not quick to make new friends.

The men lined up on the long front porch and washed one by one in a blue enameled basin beside a bucket of water. Each man soaped his hands and arms and rinsed the suds away, then splashed water on his face and dried himself on a towel hanging from a nail. The soapy water went into the dirt yard. Shirts were pulled on, hats left on the porch and hair smoothed back by damp fingers before they went inside.

Tom counted five men, two of them younger than himself, the others older. The young men talked to each other and to Weiss in what must have been German. He offered the rest his name and a handshake as they waited for their plates. The house was too small for the crowd and they took the food outside, perching on the edge of the porch after the chairs filled up. The girl was as pretty as Tom remembered, full of smiles and quick words with the men. He caught her glance now and then waiting in the line and when she handed him the plate stacked with fried meat and biscuits and a tall helping of cream peas he smiled at her and saw a quick flush of color in her face.

The porch was high enough they could sit on the deck with feet on the ground and eat off their laps, a good enough arrangement for Tom, who hadn't tasted anybody else's cooking in a long time. One of the older men roosted beside him and kept up a conversation as they ate, pushing his words out past great mouthfuls of meat. Meacham was his name.

"Scotch-Irish stock, not one of these dutchies, though they're good enough neighbors. Keep a good farm." He paused to chew. Maria came out the door with a tray full of cups. Tom smelled coffee and the misty scent of her body as she bent to put one of the cups beside him. Her hair brushed his shoulder.

"Thank you," he said, wanting to say more, to hold her attention for a second, knowing that was a fool thing to want.

She smiled in reply and moved on.

Like the others he went back for a second plate. When they finished eating they stood and sat around in the shade, groaning and laughing with full bellies. Meacham rolled a smoke and offered the makings to Tom.

"No, thanks." He fetched his pipe and brought it back to the porch shade and got it lit.

One of the young men came and sat beside him, offering his hand and his name, Alexander Kirk.

"That's a good looking horse," he said, nodding in the direction of the stallion. " Looks like a racer." His accent was heavy. He was a well-built, handsome man with blond hair and blue eyes. His face was red with sunburn.

"Well, I haven't tried him yet, but I think he'll do."

"My horse is fast."

Tom pulled on his pipe and let the smoke escape his lips. What was this? From the other end of the porch Maria and her brother were looking at him, as if he were the object of their discussion.

"Which one's yours?"

"In the pen. The dun gelding," said the stranger. Tom had noticed him when he put his mare in there and thought him a fine looking animal.

What was Kirk waiting for? Tom said, "You race him?"

The blond man's response was quick. "When there's good competition. Like your stallion." So that was it, then. The man was trying to stir up a race.

Tom drew on his pipe again. "I don't think so. Like I told you, I ain't really run him hard yet." But something else was in the air that Tom couldn't get a handle on. He saw the friendly attitude vanish from the man's face, replaced by what might be called satisfaction.

"Okay, then," Kirk said. He stood up without another word and walked the length of the porch to the place where Maria and Tobias stood. He put an arm around Maria's waist and said something to them. Tobias glanced at Tom then jerked his eyes away. Maria looked displeased.

What about Kirk's arm around the girl? Looked like he had a claim on her. Did he see Tom as a challenger?

Before Cloud could stop himself he'd called out loud enough for everybody in the yard to hear, "Kirk! Let's do it!"

CHAPTER 22

They lined the two animals up, both bareback. Tom could feel the stallion's muscles tensed under him, the quiver that ran along the black's ribcage. The other men were excited, putting down bets on the outcome, and it looked like most expected the dun to win. Understandable. Kirk was a neighbor, somebody they all knew. Meacham came up, dodging the animal's capers and said, "I like that black's looks, mister. My money's on you."

He looked around for Maria, who was the real reason for what was about to take place. She stood near Kirk's horse and did not look Tom's way. Kirk glanced toward him and said, "I'll put up five dollars against yours."

Everybody could hear the exchange. "Make it ten."

The young German waited a second, then smiled and nodded his head.

Florian Weiss strode out from the small crowd carrying a short piece of lumber. He tossed it on the ground. He said, "Behind this you start, and here you finish. You go to that far corner." He pointed at a distant place where a man stood in an angle of the stone fence. "You circle around John there, and you come back. Simple, eh?" The big gentleman seemed amused.

Tom expected the dun to get a lead on him at the start. The horse had the heavy hindquarters of a cowpony, and when Weiss yelled "Go!" that's what happened. Kirk was three lengths ahead by the time the stallion stretched out his neck and began to race. He pulled abreast before they reached the halfway angle. The dun pivoted fastest around their human marker and made up some distance, then began to fall back, and Tom knew he had it won long before they finished. He could hear the yells of encouragement, aimed not at him, but at

Kirk, and looking back saw that the Dun had faltered, dropping far behind. The stallion didn't want to quit, and Tom had to slide off and use the reins to hold him. The big runner could have gone the distance again with ease, and sure thing, he'd bought a good one.

Meacham was collecting money. Few of the men looked happy. Maria stood far apart from everyone. Kirk rode past the finish, pulling his horse down to a trot, then slid off and walked over to Tom. Tom saw the man's shoulder muscles bunch and reacted. What came at him was a wild right fist that threw Kirk off balance. Tom dodged it and could have piled into the man's belly and done him serious damage. He didn't. Bright colors flashed through his mind, the rainbow he'd found healing in. He stepped back.

"You run away?" Kirk's blond hair had fallen over his eyes. His fists were up."You scared to stand and fight me?"

Tom said, "No, sir. I'm not running, I'm not afraid, and I'm not fighting you."

What he felt mostly was embarassed. If Kirk had seen his glances at Maria then others must have, too. And all the while he'd thought his presence here, his notice of the girl, went un-remarked. Over the heads of the men paying up and collecting on their bets he found her face in the shade of the tree she leaned against, talking to her brother. She was talking to Tobias, yes, but her eyes were on him and this time she didn't tear them away. Tom couldn't place just what those eyes re-vealed, but it made him feel better, and that was good enough for now.

He led the stallion back to the horse pen and turned him inside this time, pulling the bridle loose and laying it across a rail beside the gate. Around him men were taking up their tools and laying ladders against the little building. When he walked over to the work site he saw a pile of corrugated tin, silver-gray and shiny in the afternoon sunshine, and smelled the turpentine scent of sawn lumber. He had ridden too far to stand by idle, and leaving now would seem like running. To a passing stranger he said, "Tell me what to do. I want to help."

CHAPTER 23

They'd been wrong coming back into Texas. But they had not known how many whites there were now on the land. Sage thought about the way it had been in these hills and along these rivers. And how it was now. The woman and his children slept inside the tipi, but he felt no weariness except the tiredness of disappointment, the lack of strength defeat causes you to feel. He watched the night and wondered if Yellow Bow was asleep. Probably not. But it was late and nothing moved except the water not far from the tree he sat against. It curled through boulders taller than a man and round as the moon, running fast on a shallow bottom. Somewhere in the trees a night bird sang its quick song, the notes repeating over and over again.

Across the shallow stream, up the side of a hill, among the cactus and thorn trees, in a split of limestone, wrapped in a deerskin, the old blind man lay, the pouch of pozole beside him for his journey. A pile of fieldstone hid the body and protected it from coyotes.

Sage felt sorry about the burned corn crib. The farmer had been generous and friendly, but there would have been others maybe not so friendly brought by the smoke of that fire. There might have been a fight, and blood on both sides, and then what would happen to these people of his. They were not his, but made themselves his, and were under his wings, and so he thought of them and not himself when he would rather stand and fight.

The fighting did no good. You could kill them all day and night and in the morning there would be more with their fences and plows and the new thing, the owning of the land. It was the new thing that gave him the hardest time. How could a man own the sky or the wind? Or the land under his feet?

Somewhere in the world must be a god that said who owned it, and that nobody else could own it. It was the same wherever his people tried to live. This place where they slept tonight, this river and the old man's grave, was someone else's. A white man had it, and a line was around it that you couldn't see, but inside the line that man owned it. So you couldn't stay there. But across that line was land another man owned and you couldn't plant corn there, either. The soldiers would come if you tried. If that same god said somebody else owned the air what would you breathe?

It made him want to scream and throw himself into the river. But these people had put themselves under his wings. So he would keep silent and patient, and they would go back over the Rio Bravo to Mexico. Maybe there he could sleep again.

Tom Cloud rode through Mason in the dark. Lamplight shone out of two windows and through the batwing doors of the salloon. Dogs barked and ran around nipping at the horses' legs until the stallion grew tired of it and kicked one of them and they shut up. He saw nobody.

There was starlight enough to keep them on the road. He shouldn't have left the German's hospitality like this, and he knew it and felt stupid. But that girl, and the things—the unexpected things—she'd said had made it impossible to stay there longer.

His left arm ached, overused in the work of finishing the building. They'd completed the roof while the daylight lasted, then all of the neighbors had left for home, the Kirk fellow holding back, jealous of Cloud's presence, though Florian Weiss insisted he stay for supper and wait for morning before heading out. Finally Kirk had talked with Maria alone on the porch and she had come inside alone looking sad or confused or maybe angry—he couldn't tell which. They ate food left over from midday.

Tobias carried a lantern for him to the mound of corn they'd saved out of the fire and he fed the two animals from it. When they were finished with it and had the gate shut again Tobias said in perfect English, the first time Tom had heard him speak, "Alex has asked Maria to marry him."

Cloud tried to sound like it didn't matter, but his voice came out pitched higher than he liked. "Yeah? What did she say to it?"

Tobias shrugged. His shoulders were thin, not much wider than his body. Whatever his age he looked like just a boy in the shifting light. "I think she said *maybe*."

Then later, after the men had sat on the porch, Tom and Florian Weiss smoking pipes, talking in that low almost wordless drone voices take on in the dark when men are tired from working, saying unimportant things, later after the others had gone inside and Tom had laid out his bedroll and nearly gotten to sleep, she had come.

"Thank you for not fighting with him," she said, putting it in a whisper just loud enough for him to hear. He could see nothing of her except her dark shape silhouetted against the light at the door. He strained to find a reply and failed at it.

"I saw you looking at me, but I am not free to look back. Do you understand?"

He didn't bother to match her whisper. "No. I reckon I don't."

"I'm sorry," she whispered again, and went inside and closed the door behind her.

After that, sleep held no interest for him and he did not want to see their faces in the morning. He saddled the mare and left.

With all of that, whatever it had been, settled and behind him now, alone on the road with only the sound of hoofs, he began to feel better. It was just that the girl had caused him uncertainty, that's all. One more fork in the road, and either way you took was better than trying to decide. He realized now that he'd been undecided about her from the time he saw her first that day with Lanny. Somewhere in the back of his mind had been the possibility of her, but only the possibility, gone now and his head clear. It was only one thing gone, all the rest still in front of him to get done and get lived, and he would do that. Yes, he felt much better now, and not tired any longer. He would make a dry camp somewhere ahead and let the horses rest. There was plenty of water in his canteen for coffee and he had fed well enough back there to last him all the way home.

CHAPTER 24

The mockingbird woke him a little before sunrise. The fire had died to ashes. He shivered in the morning cold, shirt and pants damp with dew and the left arm still aching. Another ache had settled into his back where he rested against the caliche bank, but it eased a little when he sat up straighter. His hat had fallen forward and covered his face and the cup of coffee he'd brewed last night stood untouched beside him. He'd gone to sleep before he could drink it.

"Hush," he said to the bird. It came out thick and unformed, but the mocker flew. He got the hat right, with his eyes blinking away sleep while he thought his way up to this moment. He stirred the ashes and found a handful of embers. He put the coffee on them and saddled the stallion. He'd staked the two horses on long ropes so they could graze close by.

The climbing and carrying and lifting of yesterday had left his muscles sore, the way long marches under heavy packs left you sore next day. A feeling of strength came along with it, though. A familiar feeling he liked. He drank the coffee while standing, enjoying the bitter heat of it on his tongue and down his throat and spreading in his stomach where the chill had been.

It wasn't until he'd mounted and ridden back to the road leading the mare that he let himself remember the girl and how he'd felt on the ride up here and the day past, and now the ride back home. It was like an experience from a distant past that you could remember clearly but did not feel.

Two hours later a thin stream of water slid down a hillside a hundred yards off the road like another traveler come to join him. Cottonwoods and Spanish oaks fed on the water and grew tall over it. He watered the horses in the shade and filled his canteen and heard a gunshot far to the south. A second one, then silence again. A squirrel barked in one of the trees above his head.

He met a lone horseman and later a wagon pulled by mules, two men on the bench of the wagon, a squeal in one of the wheels that caused his horses to shy away and the bed of it loaded with cargo covered by canvas. All on their way toward Mason. He remembered the gunshots and thought about asking the rider, then the men in the wagon, about them, but didn't stop for it, just offered a friendly wave and went on. He reined the black horse off the road at the big live oak he'd left standing in his mind as a marker and a turning point and knew he'd be home by the middle of the afternoon.

This stretch of hills held no fences. A few longhorned cattle grazed where the grass grew thick and small flocks of goats and sheep watched from a distance or ran, wild as the deer that fed among them. The day was heating up, but the sun felt weightless on his back and shoulders, and he was glad to be here in this place riding these good horses that he trusted through country not quite tamed. He smelled smoke. Just a taste of it, nowhere close, but on the wind coming uphill from the south. Branding fire, maybe. He thought of that day with Lanny and guided the black out of the open and into the edge of the cedar brake growing thick close by. He pulled the Henry out of its sheath and laid it across the saddle in front of his hips.

Another half mile or so and he heard sounds, nothing distinct enough that he could identify it, a hum that could have been part of spoken words. The smoke was stronger now and the smell of cooking meat was in it. His mouth watered and he remembered he hadn't had anything to eat since the night before. He led the horses farther into the cedars and tied them.

He made a careful circuit down the hill. The hum turned into words as he got closer. Two men were talking in Spanish. He had no idea what they were saying but it didn't sound friendly.

On his knuckles and knees, holding the Henry by barrel and stock, he found a vacant spot between two of the bushy trees,

92

cedar needles stinging his face and hands, and saw men with rifles standing in a half-circle around two Indians, Apaches by the look of them. Three women and two boys, one of them half-grown, watched the men. A little cooking fire gave off the smoke he had first noticed. A black pot hung over it. Boiling meat, probably.

The white men looked familiar, and when he recognized the captain, he realized who they were. They'd found their Apaches, all right.

Cloud moved back to a live oak and stood behind it just in case anybody decided to shoot, and called out.

"Captain Grant!"

There was general talk and movement and the snap of rifles. "Who's that? Show yourself!"

"It's Tom Cloud, Captain! The pecan trees, down on the creek?"

"I remember you! Come on out. We won't fire on you!"

He guessed maybe he wouldn't get shot, so he walked on out into the open with the Henry pointed at the ground.

The ranger who'd been talking to the Apache took up the conversation again as Tom walked over. He heard Grant say, "Tell him to go on and eat, then. No point in starving them. But you men look around and see if there's any weapons hid away. And make us some coffee on that fire of theirs."

Closer now, Tom said, "I heard gunshots a while back."

Grant met him with a handshake and a thin smile. "Yes, we sent them a salute to kind of introduce ourselves." Grant looked worn down since Tom had last seen the man. His clothes were dirty and a beard had a good start on his face.

"Nobody hurt?"

"No, sir. This is no war party. It's mostly women and kids. We shot in the air and they showed a white flag. We took our time with it, though. You can't tell about these boogers. They can trick you into getting massacred if you don't watch out."

"I've been up at the Weiss place above Mason." He told Grant the story.

The captain grinned and shook his head. "This is the same bunch, I'll bet."

"Weiss thought the head man's name was Sage, or something like it."

"It's them, all right. Sage it is, the tall one Felipe was talking to."

They walked toward the fire and the mix of white and Indian around it, the boys eating at chunks of meat from the pot, the adults standing back, out of the sun and still, watching it all in stunned wariness. Tom thought them a good looking people. The women were pretty, the two men wide-shouldered and strong in appearance.

Grant said, "Felipe, ask him if they're the ones had the old man die."

When the Mexican posed the question Tom saw their eyes register surprise. The man named Sage nodded his head.

A couple of the rangers brought cups and handed coffee around. Tom declined.

"No, my cup's up the hill with my horses. You men go ahead."

"There's plenty for everybody," Grant said. "Take one. And Felipe—see if the two Apaches want some. We've got to figure out what to do with these wayward folks." He gathered the men around him away from the Indians. Tom gathered with them, interested in the outcome, glad it was not his decision. These looked like harmless, decent people, and they were about to be herded like a flock of goats to some godforsaken reservation. Grant seemed to be a good-hearted person, but he would have duty in front of him. The Mexican stayed with Sage and the other Indian, talking to them in a low voice while they drank from the cups he had given them.

Grant kept his good humor, but a few of his men did not. "Let's just shoot the vermin," somebody said. "While we're playin' nursemaid there's depredation goin' on elsewhere."

The captain fixed a hard gaze on the speaker. "Dempsey, I see you in church on Sundays. I don't believe that is a Christian sentiment." The man's face turned red. Grant went

94

on. "No, we won't shoot them. I see nothing else except to escort them up to Fort Mason and keep them under guard there while we scout some more. Anybody else got a better idea?"

Nobody did.

But something nudged at Tom Cloud for the next hour, while he went up the hill for his horses and came back to watch the people gather the camp and load the pack animals. Militiamen stood about chewing tobacco and joking in low voices. It was the time after battle. None had taken place here, but that was just luck. They'd all been up for it, ready for it, and now they joked, but they stayed ready.

The two Lipan men moved around in silence. Tom watched the one called Sage walk over to a boy and touch him on the shoulder. The boy had on a brave face, but his lips trembled. It would be shameful for him if he showed fear among these whites. *We're the ones ought to feel shame,* Tom thought to himself.

It nudged him some more when the translator gave Sage orders to mount up, speaking to him in Spanish and getting a hard, dark look from the Indian. Then, before you could see it happen Sage had a knife in his hand and his arm around Felipe's neck, using him as a shield with the shining blade against his throat.

CHAPTER 25

Grant stepped forward, motioning to the others to settle down. "Keep your hands off your guns, gentlemen. Felipe has a fine tenor voice I'd like to preserve."

Tom heard the man named Dempsey again. "Like I told you, Captain, it's better we just shoot 'em, get it done."

"Any more of that, sir, and I'll have your resignation. Understood?"

Most of the others looked like they agreed with Dempsey. Sage spoke to his people in a low, controlled voice and they moved to obey him, mounting up and leading the pack horses away. The militia still had their guns, and no way would the Apaches get them back. What chance did the Indians have? Sage backed up, pulling the unresisting Felipe along, the knife always at the man's throat.

Grant put up his empty hands as if he might use them to draw the people back, stop what was going to happen here. "Sage," he said, "No. No." The Indian spit words back at him from lips curled down, thin and tight and angry.

Grant put his hand to his ear. "No comprende. I don't understand. Let Felipe speak. What does he say?"

Felipe twisted his neck and drew in air. " The others go. He stays." It was to be an act of sacrifice, then. The big man figured to die, but not until the others were safe away. Safe for a little while, anyhow.

Tom heard someone behind him cock a pistol. There was a hiss in the air, then a grunt of surprise and he turned to see Dempsey flat on the ground, his pistol in his hand and a blunt arrow, the sort of arrow the Lipans used for rabbits, on the ground beside his head. The boy whose lips had trembled sat astride his horse, a short bow in his left hand and a look of fierceness on his face. The idea that had nudged Tom sprang up full blown. He thought it might be the only way to stop what was sure to happen.

"Captain Grant," he said, and stepped forward.

It took half an hour to get Felipe's neck out of the Indian's grip. First, Tom had to tell Grant what he had in mind, from the first idea to what he'd finally worked out. And all along not knowing if it was sensible or just plain crazyness. First off, all he knew about Sage for sure was that he was quick with a knife. It was just Weiss's word that the man wasn't bloodthirsty. But the look on the young boy's face, the tremble in his lips and the way he fought to be manly, the way Sage had gone to the boy and touched him on the shoulder. All of that meant something. Maybe it couldn't be wrapped up in words, but you could feel it. Tom felt it.

After that it took Grant a while to come around and agree. And he didn't agree until he'd talked to all his men. Some were quick to give a yes. A few kicked at the ground with a boot toe, not willing to go along with it, but understanding it might be for the best. Dempsey sat alone and held his head in his hands.

A scared Felipe had to listen to it and try to explain it to Sage, thinking that any minute the knife could split his windpipe and end it all.

Tom watched the big Apache's face. Nothing moved across it, nothing changed in the twist of his mouth or the sure intention of his knife hand. The others in the bunch had gone a little way off and stopped under shade. But finally, finally, the dark eyes flew at Tom and quickly away, back on the man he held. Sage took in a deep breath and let it out, then slowly removed the knife and then opened his arm and allowed Felipe to walk away. The Mexican's knees gave out after two or three steps and Grant got his elbow, then guided him to a seat on a downed log.

Sage held the knife then, by its blade, and walked toward Tom, extending it, wanting him to take it. It seemed safe enough. Tom reached for it, then turned it around and gave it back. He hoped Sage understood that he would trust him. And he hoped that the trust was not misplaced.

He could hear them behind him on the ride home, their low voices, their grunts, and now and then a short laugh. The travois poles they used to carry their tipis dragged over the rocky ground with a scraping sound that made his teeth hurt. He would have been home hours before if he hadn't opened his mouth back there. Now the late shadows stretched and night would soon be coming on. He'd have to get them bedded before dark.

The boy bagged three squirrels out of the trees with his blunt arrows while the Apache women took the travois poles off their horses and stacked them into tipi poles that they arranged beside the creek a few hundred yards south of his cabin. The two warriors, Sage and the other man, watched the work from a shady spot and seemed uninclined to talk with him. Well, he didn't know the Spanish or Apache tongues anyway, and they didn't appear to know any English, either, so how much talking they might do was a question mark anyhow. The boy carried his squirrels to the youngest woman and threw them on the grass at her feet. She smiled at him and picked them up and carried them to the creek edge. She produced a knife from out of her clothing and began to skin the animals.

That would be supper, then, Cloud guessed, and wondered at a hunter who didn't dress his own kills. Let the boy be, though. Let the young rascal have all the squirrels he could harvest. They had to be gotten rid of if he was going to depend on the pecans for a livelihood.

Twilight turned grayer and the sun was a red eyebrow just at the horizon when the two older women began unrolling skins and lifting them up to cover the tipi poles. They were tired and struggled with the heavy skins. The two men made no move to help. The young woman finished cleaning the squirrels, washed them in the creek and washed her hands and the knife, then found a cloth or a skin—he couldn't tell in the growing dark— that she spread on the ground and put the meat on it. She brought in sticks of wood and built a fire, then hung the same iron pot over it. Looked like supper was going to be squirrel stew.

Cloud walked over to the women and took hold of one end of a heavy deer hide. It was more than one, he discovered; three or four of them, stitched together. He lifted it and held it in place, the stink of it like grease and smoke while the women finished attaching it to the skeleton of poles. They did not look at him or acknowledge his help in any way. He began to feel embarrassed, and left them to finish. He gathered his horses, remembered a few words of Spanish, said "Buenos noches" and led his animals to their pen. The shadows beneath the pecan trees had turned full dark. He could no longer see the two Apache men, and no one returned his good night.

He had not expected gratitude from them and doubted they truly understood why he had intervened in their lives. To be honest he didn't understand it, either, and he thought about the situation as he worked his way between trees and around the few stands of underbrush and cactus that managed to live in the shadow of the trees. The two horses came along easily. He carried saddle and tack to the cabin and came back with a bucket of oats, reminding himself that he had to build a shed to hold feed and tools and whatever else might be needed. The night was dark and he did it all by feel, the homestead already a familiar place to his feet and hands. A soft breeze brought the smell of cooking meat. He was hungry, but darned if he'd beg off the Indians, even if it was his squirrel. He went inside, found matches and lit the coal oil lantern.

With the soft kerosene flames bouncing on the walls it seemed all of a sudden a friendly place. Not home; not yet, anyway, but he felt glad to be there. He hadn't left much food around when he took off on his trip, figuring he would watch for deer on the return. Still, there were four covered crocks along one wall, and nothing had disturbed them. One held flour, another cornmeal, a third one was filled to the top with dried beans, and the fourth held venison he had sliced thin and smoked over an oak fire. The meat looked okay and smelled okay. He bit off a piece and found that it tasted fine. Better than fine. He was hungry. It took a while to start a fire in the little hearth and fry some cornmeal mush to go with the jerky, and when it was ready he ate quickly, thinking again of the Indians and wondering again just what he would propose to them in the morning.

The best thing he could think of, and what he'd promised the militia, was to let them stay right there and wait until things calmed down, then escort them south and across the border. If he was along, then settlers would be slow to attack them. Maybe. And if the Apaches didn't want to do that, there was always a reservation and plenty of white men willing to put them on it.

He boiled coffee and leaned back in his poor excuse for a bunk, sipping at the bitter brew and feeling sleepy.

The cup was hot. He set it down, careful not to spill it. He shut his eyes and dozed. Time went by. He was half-asleep, half-awake. A loud voice called out.

"Anybody inside the cabin?" Tom reached for his gunbelt and slid the long pistol out of its holster. He moved along the wall and stood next to the latched door. Whoever was out there couldn't get to him without knocking the door down and he felt safe enough with the big .45 in his hand.

"Hello? I see some light in there. I mean no harm."

The voice seemed familiar, but he couldn't place it. Tom said, "What do you want?"

"Sorry to come hollering in the dark like this. I'm looking for a feller by the name of Tom Cloud. You happen to know him?"

"Well, who are..." And then he remembered the voice, and the banty walk, and the wounded cowboy he'd left behind many a month ago.

CHAPTER 26

The lantern light showed the little man thinner, casting shadows on skin nearer the bone, the sunken cheeks and deeper eyes of someone who'd touched the edge of death. The mustache was not quite as full, but hung in place just the same, and the smile under it was as bright and genuine as ever.

Tom shook the reaching hand and brought him inside, trying for words and finding none, some barely-remembered feeling of joy hammering through him. He heard himself say finally, "What..." And that was all. Nothing behind it. Lanny's smile got bigger.

"I smell grease. You got anything for a starving man?"

They watered and fed the bay gelding and left him grazing on a long rope. "Charlie is a friendly sort and that black of yours is acting offended. Lets leave him outside the pen tonight."

Tom said, "He's not too bad for a stallion, but that's best for now. Maybe they can get acquainted better in daylight."

Lanny ate perched on Tom's cot. Between bites he talked. "Not much to tell about for a long time after I got shot. Gruntin' and sleepin' is about it. They took good care of me back at the Bigboy, though. Can't complain about the nursin'." He blew across the top of his coffee to cool it and drank some of it. "I figured all along I'd die from it, but as things turned out I did not."

"I ran out on you."

Tom's words halted the story. Lanny looked at him without speaking for a long time while shadows and light tiptoed around the walls. "Loretta Sterns told me how you was feelin' about what happened."

"I was ashamed. Still am. I'm sorry."

"For what? Not gettin' shot?"

"I killed a man." He went back to his coffee.

Lanny sayed silent for a minute, then said, "We fought the war. Men died. No shame in that."

"No, after the war, in a match. I'd fought no tellin' how many times, always won, always walked away with money in my hand. Then this man. His name was O'Keefe. Big Irishman, and a good boxer, too. He just dropped dead coming out for the second round."

"I'd say that was an accident, not your fault."

"That's right, it wasn't, but for a long time it seemed like it was. I couldn't get over it. I quit and went running and ended up here."

"That's what caused it all, then. Messed up your thinkin'."

"It did that, all right."

"But you got over it? You're okay now?" Lanny poured himself more coffee, then emptied the pot into Tom's cup.

He told the rest of it—the unexpected cowardice, the flight from self-blame, the branding and the healing, the coming to this place and his unwillingness to be run from it.

Lanny forgot to eat. "I knew you was carrying a load, all right, just didn't know how heavy it was." He swallowed more coffee. "Just so it is clear to you, I ain't never blamed you for a thing, and I won't have you blaming yourself over it. I got to know you a little in that line cabin we wintered in, and I think of you as a friend. None of it was your fault."

There is no fault. Tom remembered the Mexican girl, the turn of her mouth, her insistence. The rainbow. He smiled. "I know that now. What I don't know is how you managed to find me."

"I do believe I could hire out to Pinkerton if ever I quit the range. It seemed logical to me that you might've wandered out this way. I went up to Mason, which is the toehold of civilization around here and looked at the land records, thinking you may have settled down. And there it was. I waltzed on down this direction and come across a couple of fellers herdin' sheep. Some people will do anything to make a livin', I guess. Well, they sent me to an old woman name of Schneider, who fed me tea and pointed south. And here I am.

According to that little old lady, you're planted smack in the middle of a feud."

"You've quit the Bigboy, then."

"Oh, no. I'm goin' back after awhile. Ain't really fit for workin' cows right now, and I wanted to tell you what I just told you and get you thinkin' right. Loretta Sterns enouraged it and sends her best. She liked you. Rudy did, too."

"Something I didn't mention about that bunch of militiamen. One of 'em was named Crenshaw."

The little rooster smiled. "That's another reason for my journey."

"And I didn't mention the Apaches. You probably saw 'em camped out yonder on the creek."

Lanny stared at him and then swallowed more coffee. "I come up the creek," he said, "but I sure didn't see nobody else."

They walked through the trees, the swinging lantern just enough to light the way, most of it lost in the leaves and brush. They found a circle of ash with a few embers still glowing, marks on the ground where the tipi had stood, and nothing else.

"Redmen is clever folks," Lanny said. He dropped a cud of snuff under his lip.

Tom felt nothing much except tired. "Let's get some sleep," he said.

CHAPTER 27

His horse was weary. So was he. Sage knew they had to stop and rest. Soon morning would come and with it maybe the militia again. He had to find a good hiding place, sheltered from the light rain that had begun falling. They couldn't put up the tipis, although the skins were rolled up and stacked on the backs of two horses. The travois poles they'd left behind, in tall grass near the creek. The scrape of those poles was too easy to track. They could cut more poles once they made it back safely to the mountains of Mexico. A place they never should have left.

He hoped he'd led his people far enough west to miss the settlers of Bexar. The rocky ground in the strip of hill country was hard for the soldiers to track through. And there were caves and cliffs and hidden places. It bothered him a little that he had broken his word to the white man. But, as everyone knew, the word of a white man was no good anyway. That piece of ground the white man called his own, the big trees, the creek of sweet water, had belonged to the Apache people since before memory. Their bones were in the dirt of the place. He could not stay there as a beggar.

Sage, alone, could have reached the border in a day or two of hard riding on a fresh horse. Now, even with luck, it would still take twice as long with the women and the need to travel carefully.

What did that white man want, anyway? To keep him as a pet? Like a dog you feed and give shelter to? Like a prize pony you show to friends? He could see the form of his son, the young fellow slumped over the mane of his horse, a shadow among shadows, only a boy, but with much courage and obedience. A boy who deserved equal courage from his father. Sage sat up straighter and stared into the night, watching for a camping spot.

Tom Cloud and his friend waited for the coffee to boil. Tom could hear conversation between his stallion and Lanny's bay gelding. Their grunts and insults filtered through the cabin walls. Like two little boys in a schoolyard. It was a rainy day, water finding its way through his makeshift roof of saplings thatched with cedar branches and onto the two men, the bed, Lanny's blanket roll, everything inside. Tom put an empty crock under the worst drip. The rain had livened up the squirrels in his trees, and their sharp barks filled the empty spaces in the noise of the two horses. Sounded like a church choir trying to get tuned up.

"Fool way to live," he said. "A man needs a good roof." He filled the crooked pipe and lit it.

Lanny lifted the pot and poured two cups of the brown, hot stuff. He handed one to Tom. "We goin' after your Apaches?"

"I don't want to. Hard to believe I was dumb enough to bring 'em here."

"Aw, Tom, you just got that need to save the world from its badness, I think. Might work sometimes. Didn't work this time." He blew on his coffee and swallowed a mouthful, squinting against the heat of it. "Them militia ain't goin' to like it, though. Let's us go drag 'em back and save your skin."

"Could be hard to do. Sage is a tough one. That Yellow Bow, too. Don't know I'd want to go man to man on either one. And you just out of the sickbed. I wouldn't want to see you get hurt all over again." Tom bent over the fire and lifted the lid of a pot he'd left on the coals overnight. The smell of cooked beans steamed up.

Lanny said, "You ain't got to worry about me, Tom. I'm here to help. And I believe some fried squirrel would go good with them pintos. Hold still and I'll be right back."

The rock overhead held off the rain. They ate the last of the stew cooked beside the white man's creek last night. The camp lay next to a narrow river with high banks cut into the rocky

108

soil, its current pointed southeast. Sage didn't know this country, or this river, but it was water for them and the horses, they had shelter for a while, and they all needed rest. It looked shallow enough. He'd find a good crossing later and they could continue farther west.

"If we can find game we will stay here today and tonight," he told his wife. "This rain will end before tomorrow." He saw something white in her hand. A piece of curved bone. A fishhook.

"Don't worry about your belly, husband. I see fish in that river."

The boy walked upstream until the steep wall dropped lower, then climbed out of the riverbed. He walked back until he was above the camp and could smell the smoke from the small fire below. He swung himself into an oak tree with his bow slung over his shoulder and three arrows held tight in his left hand. He shinnied higher until he could see the land roundabout. The rain peppered his face, but he didn't mind it, so long as it didn't soak his bowstring He always carried the bow and the arrows, but he had not come to hunt. Sage had sent him here to watch. To keep the people safe. He sat still and watched for a long time. The rain got harder. His bowstring became limp and useless, and that caused in him a helpless feeling. Not one a warrior should feel.

No pursuers came. He sniffed at the thin smoke drifting past and caught the smell of cooking. He was hungry and it was the middle of the day. It wouldn't take long to go down there and eat a little and then come back. He spent time gazing at the distant hills, saw nothing moving and made up his mind. Then, as he turned to begin climbing off the tree, he looked north, where the river came from, and he saw something that, as brave as he was, frightened him. His mouth dried up and inside his chest a quick pounding began. He dropped to the ground, ignoring the sharp pain in his feet and legs, and ran to the edge of the riverbed. He couldn't see anyone because of the overhanging rock. It was too late to go down. He began to yell a warning at the top of his voice.

The river was not very wide, and the walls on both sides were steep and high. Rain farther upcountry had filled creeks and shallow tributaries and run into the river for many miles up and down it, filling it up and raising it higher. The excess water had no place to go except downstream. It came rushing now, with no warning, no noise, curling out and slapping at the cliffsides like an angry bear. The boy heard shouts below. Maybe he had warned them in time. The wall of water hit and flew past, so high that he could have dived in easily if he had been a fool.

And then the huge rise dropped. It was just a river again. Far below the place he stood. The horses squealed somewhere in the distance. The river had them, he knew. His father, his mother, his sister? What about them? He began to run, slipping in the alkaline mud and falling hard, then getting up and going on, back the way he had come, very afraid of what he would find.

CHAPTER 28

The rain was a bother, but it was a blessing, too, because the damp ground showed up the hoofprints of the Indian's horses. Tom said, "They'll stop there, I bet. At the river. We can catch up to 'em."

"I don't know, Tom. Them people nearabout live on horse-back and they ride hard. They may just plain outrun us."

Tom was on his Apaloosa mare. He'd left the stallion in the little corral. Alone for the first time since Tom bought him, he had griped until they were out of sight, begging to go along. The mare was a better choice in this weather and rainslick footing. The rain fell harder. All the two men could do was pull their slickers tighter and hurry on before the tracks they followed washed away and left them without direction.

The boy pulled off his moccasins and went on barefoot through the mud left behind by the great pulse of water. He heard nothing but the sounds of the flowing river and the fall of rain. And in his heart he carried a dread that seemed to wrap itself around his throat and squeeze until he could hardly breathe. Then something moved just ahead, where the camp had been. Someone in the mud. His mother? Yes. She moved again, her legs twisting, trying to push herself upright. She looked bad, like she had fought a battle, and she was soaked in mud, her head and shoulders caught in a split between two boulders, caught there and so the river couldn't carry her farther. But she lived.

It was not easy getting her free of the rocks that held her. Neither spoke as they struggled. On her feet at last she stared around them with questions in her eyes, but no words yet. Understanding had not yet made its way into her thinking. The boy led her to a river rock large enough to sit on. She turned her head suddenly and looked at the water and then stood again and started to walk away.

"They are gone," he said. "The river took them."

"No." She shook her head, but her voice had dropped into a moan, and she knew it was true. The rain was just a drizzle now, and clouds over their heads were breaking up, a little sunshine glancing down. They heard a shout downriver.

Just short of the bend, on the western side, a gradual slope came down from the plain above and extended into the water. Cypress trees grew there, reaching out into the river and holding solid, their knees raising up around each tree and creating a dark, wet mass of growing things in the accumulated silt and eroded soil from above. Halfway up the trunks of the great trees was a straight line of grasses, branches, small logs, brought by the flash flood and others like it, caught there and held as the rocks had held his mother. In one of the trees, high up among the graceful branches, movement.

The boy's eyes were very good. He watched the spot where something had moved. A face came out of the green Cypress needles. A hand wiped at the face. "My father," he said. And though his voice was the calm voice of a warrior, his heartbeat was that of a young boy whose world had been lost and was found again.

"No. He is gone."

"It's Sage. Look." He pointed and she saw the face he pointed to.

"Can we save him?"

"He is hurt, I think, or he would come down off that tree. The river is slower now. I'll swim it and try to bring him back."

"No, you are only a child."

"Mother, you say often that I am a child, and you forget I am Sage's child." He placed the useless bow on the rock where they stood, and the three arrows and his moccasins beside it. He took five running steps and dove into the river.

The current was much stronger than he'd thought. In the center of the river it turned him around and tumbled him feet over head as if he were nothing more than a floating log. The water that had run clear the day before was muddy now, full of white foam, a silty brew of leaf and twig and flakes of limestone that pushed him down. His nose and mouth filled with it and he fought against the intake of imagined breath that would drown him. Felt his right shoulder scrape against rock bottom, put his feet against it and shoved upward.

When he burst above the surface he spit out the water and sucked air fast and deep, sure he'd be forced under again, but the hard current swung away from the grove of Cypress and set him free and he was able to go on to the shore. He grabbed a Cypress knee and held himself there, out of breath and weak from the struggle. His ears were plugged with water and he could hear nothing.

Time passed and he remembered again his reason for being there. He pulled himself forward among the stand of trees to a place where his feet touched bottom and he rose up waist-high above the water. Debris was piled everywhere, blocking his way. He looked into the treetops and felt water drain from his left ear. He tilted his head and cleared the right one, and could hear again, and what he heard was Sage calling to him.

He waded among the trees and their knees and the mounds of captured washoff. One of the mounds had built itself around a horse, upside down, its legs in the air.

"See if the rope is on my horse's leg," Sage called down. "He was hobbled with a long rope."

It was there, all right, but the knot was wet and couldn't be undone. He had no knife to cut it with, or sharp stone, and saw nothing that would do it.

Sage called out. "Here is my knife. Don't try to catch it, but watch where it falls and find it." It dropped into the river close by, and the boy found it quickly, running his hands along the bottom until his right hand swept over the sharp blade. When he lifted it out of the water he saw that he had nicked the palm of his right hand. Pink stain ran down his wrist. He rinsed the hand in the river and washed away the blood and when he looked at it again the bleeding had stopped. He sliced through

113

the knot and slowly got the long hobble rope coiled and under control.

"Put it beside the tree and bring an end up with you."

"Are you hurt, Father?"

"Yes, but I'll live. Is my rifle with the horse?"

The boy waded to the dead animal and pulled some of the wastepile away. "No. The saddle is gone." He cut off the ruined knot and looped the rope around his waist. The cypress trunk was so thick he couldn't get his legs around it, but a low branch weighted down by water hung near enough to reach. He chinned himself up and over it, then scooted closer to the trunk, and he reached Sage that way, from one of the branches to the next higher.

Sage's face was covered with drying blood as if he'd been mauled by some wild animal, scratches deep into his flesh. "I think I broke my leg," he said. "I am very glad to see you, son."

They built a harness with the rope and looped the free end over a branch above their heads. The man then lowered himself to the water and the boy went down as he had come, branch to branch. Sage braced himself against a tree, standing on his good right leg and freed the rope.

"I can't walk," he said, and told his son what had to be done and how they would do it.

They looped the rope under his arms and he lay down on his belly. The boy tied the other end around his waist again and walked a few feet ahead, carrying the excess rope and pulling Sage against the current, up stream. Opposite the place their camp had been, where the anxious woman stood waiting, the cliff rose up and there was no shallow bed to walk on.

"I can help here," Sage said. "Just paddle ahead with one arm and hold onto the rope. Stay close to the wall til we get above the camp, then the current will carry us down and across to the other bank."

It happened just as he said it would. They slid the injured man out of the water and got him seated on a boulder. The boy watched as his parents embraced without speaking. There was a sense of relief and quiet pride, but there was sadness, too, because his sister and the others were gone, carried downriver and probably killed by the flood. Before the woman bent to care for the injured leg she touched her son's shoulder and said, "You are not a child."

CHAPTER 29

Tom Cloud and Lanny saw the river surge almost clear of its banks, full of broken limbs and half-rotted tree trunks, whole thorny bushes ripped out of the ground they grew in and carried into the stampeding current. Both horses shied away from the sound and sight of it. The men dismounted and held onto their reins, talked in low voices to the animals until the water dropped and the great fist of destruction went around a bend downstream.

"There's people will suffer from that, I expect," Tom said.

"Some will. Some always do, seems like."

They climbed aboard again, the horses quiet now. Lanny was staring at something behind them. He said, "When we get back I'll help you rebuild your horse pen."

"What are you...?" The black stallion was coming toward them at a slow trot.

The little man said, "Yeah, it's got a great big hole in it."

Tom put him on a lead rope behind his mare and kept a fair distance from Lanny and the gelding as they followed the river. More aggravation, and he wondered for the hundredth time if he'd made a mistake buying the stallion. Behind his doubts, though, was the gut knowledge that he had never put into words, even to himself. The time would come when the big horse's speed would be needed. When his very life might depend on those long legs. And besides, Alexander Kirk still owed him ten dollars. He remembered the voice of the girl that night on the dark porch telling him she could not look back. She never said she didn't want to, though. Maybe...no, that was a fool's dream and he would not be a fool again. They rode on, the stallion and Lanny's gelding trading insults every little while. Time moved, but it was slow and the day went on.

The rain had gone for good and dark had begun to settle in. He rode closer to Lanny.

"What do you think? Maybe we ought to find a spot to camp. Away from this muddy ditch."

Lanny kept looking straight ahead, like he hadn't heard the question, then he raised his arm and pointed. It was a dim flicker far downriver, like a match about to go out. Both men reached for their rifles and spurred the tired horses into a trot.

It was just three of them, the boy and a woman, his mother, standing in front of—shielding—the one called Sage. Sage lay on the ground behind them, in the partial protection of rocks that had been gathered and piled up to form a backdrop for the fire. The fire looked doubtful, feeding on wet sticks. The man was hurt or dead. He didn't move as they rode up. The woman looked like she'd been dragged through mud. The boy held his bow and some blunt arrows, but it was useless and the three of them had no defense. The boy laid down his weapons and picked up a handful of small rocks. He waited.

"Looks like that flash flood got 'em," Tom said.

Lanny spoke out to them in Spanish. Tom was surprised. He shoved the Henry back into its sheath. "Didn't know you could speak it."

"Little bit. Enough for now, anyway. Told 'em we was friends."

They lit off the mounts and walked toward the fire. The boy drew back to throw. The woman stared past them with no expression on her face.

"He didn't believe you. Tell him again."

"Amigos," Lanny said, and followed that with a string of talk Tom couldn't follow. They waited, and after a minute or so the woman seemed to come to herself as if waking from sleep. She put a hand on the boy's shoulder and motioned them forward with the other. She said some things to Lanny in a voice without inflection or hope.

"His leg's broke, she says. Gone into a fever and she's got no way to help him. Everything swept downriver. The others, too.

All gone, one of 'em her daughter."

The boy seemed to understand finally that the men wanted to help. He stood aside. They knelt beside the unconscious Apache. Tom ran his hands over Sage's legs. He felt the break. "It feels bad. Like the ends don't meet. If we're not careful they may poke out through his skin, and I expect he'd die for sure out here like this."

"Need to reset the bone, I guess," Lanny said. "I've done it a time or two, but we got to have splints to keep it in place."

Tom carried his big knife into the dark away from the firelight. A few stars hung over them and a thin moon was on the horizon. Enough to help him find some slender tree limbs. He cut a half dozen and carried them back. They measured the length of Sage's leg and trimmed the branches to fit him.

They had to cut off the left leg of his trousers. "Hate to do this," Tom said. "May be all he's got."

"It's do it or let him die."

Even though he was unconscious, the pain must have been great because the Indian cried out when they pulled the leg straight so that the bones could settle into place again. They cut thin strips of cloth out of the cut-off pants leg and used them to bind the splints in place against the stricken leg.

Tom put his slicker on the ground against the rock pile with the lining up and they laid Sage on it, pulling the edges together to cover him. Lanny unrolled his bedding and put the damp blanket over that. They brought in more wood and built up the fire until it began to put out real heat. Tom got the dried venison out of his saddlebag and gave it to the woman and boy. Lanny found a pot in his own gear and poured it full of water from a spare canteen and they boiled coffee. When it was ready they filled their cups and found places to sit near the fire. They drank the hot coffee and waited for morning.

CHAPTER 30

The sky was empty when the sun lit up the countryside. The river down below moved along as untroubled as it had for all the years of its past. The thousands, the tens of thousands of years. The horses grazed. Lanny leaned sleeping against a corner of the rock pile. The boy slept that way too, at the other corner, holding his bow and the blunt arrows across his chest. The woman stood over her husband who was not conscious still. The Apache's broken leg stuck straight out along the ground, wrapped tight against movement by the splint they'd built for him.

Tom felt used up, stiff and sore from the long ride and the cold rain and the hours of upright dozing by the tired little fire. He forced himself onto his feet and went to look at Sage, afraid he'd find him dead. But no, he'd made it to morning. The big man's chest moved in an even rhythm. The woman nodded, like she knew what he was thinking. He tried to smile, but his face didn't work. He was chilled all through. He put his hand on Sage's forehead and felt the fevered heat.

He heard Lanny behind him, putting the pot on the fire and smelled the coffee beginning to heat. His throat felt full of gravel. He said, "We've got to find help for this man, or he's liable to die on us."

Lanny came to stand beside him, saying nothing, the smell of smoke coming off him. He put snuff under his lip and got it shifted into place and after a little while said in what came out a whisper, "You see any? Help, I mean."

Cloud couldn't keep from a tight grin. "You remember the people took care of me I told you about?"

Lanny lifted his hat and ran his left hand across the top of his head then put the hat back down and turned to spit into the fire.

He raked his teeth across his bottom lip. "The old Meskin woman?"

"They're here somewhere, I think. Be close to a mission. The girl learned to talk English at one, she said." He watched his friend think about it.

"That ain't much guidance." Same whisper.

"You got a sore throat?"

He laughed and said louder, "Naw, just tired. You worked me hard, and I ain't rested up from finding you yet, either." He turned to the fire again and sent another stream into it. "There's missions all over the place out here."

"I guess we could turn around and take him back home. Maybe get a doctor from Mason or somewhere else. He'd be out of the weather, anyhow."

Lanny nodded. "Take a couple days, but it's a better idea than wanderin' south with no destination in mind." He spoke to the woman who stepped back, shook her head and pointed downriver. They passed some talk back and forth that Tom didn't understand. He could tell it wasn't going Lanny's way.

"Well sir," the little man said to Tom. "She's got her heels dug in. Don't know if her daughter's dead or alive and won't leave til we find out." The loud talk had waked the boy, who sat up and checked his bow string. It hadn't dried out yet, but chances were good that it would before the day ended.

Tom didn't like it. Didn't like having to nursemaid these people. Felt like turning around and heading for home and letting them do the best they could. And then he knew he was thinking crazy, thinking not like himself at all. They were in this mess because of him, anyway. If he'd left the militia alone to do their jobs none of it would have happened. He stared at the muddy ground beside his feet until he could get his feelings back where they belonged.

It took half the morning to break camp. The Indian woke up enough to help when they loaded him onto the saddle. He got one foot into a stirrup and hung the broken leg down the left side of the mare. Lanny got his hands under the woman's arms and helped her settle in behind Sage so she could hold him in

122

place and reach around him for the reins.

"I reckon it was fortunate your stallion decided to join us," he said to Tom. "Nobody's got to walk, anyway. Some of that meat's left from last night. You hungry?"

"Give it to the boy. I'll starve with the rest of you."

"We can harvest a jackrabbit or two along the way." He lifted the young Apache onto his gelding and got himself seated, watching Tom climb onto the bare back of the stallion. His Henry sat in its scabbard under the squaw's leg, and that bothered him some, but she didn't seem the sort to use it and he didn't want to carry it in his lap all day.

"That piggin' string don't make much of a bridle."

The thin leather strip was wrapped around the big black's nose and was all Tom had to control him with. He agreed with Lanny. It didn't *feel* like much of a bridle, either. He'd carried that string since the day of the branding, stuffed in his shirt pocket; carried it without thinking of how or when he would use it, but knowing a time would come. Maybe this was the time. Maybe not.

It was slow, following the river down country. They could see the water, see the wreckage of the flash flood where it had left broken trees and bushes along the banks. At places where the channel cut deep with cliffs rising up from it, they stopped and the boy went down to look for dead horses, people, clothing, anything that might begin telling the story of the lost ones. They found no signs.

The sun was overhead when they stopped to build a fire and roast the jackrabbit that had been a little too curious for his own good and a little too slow to run. The boy had tried an arrow from behind Lanny, but it fell short and Lanny used his .44. He hit the animal in the forequarters and messed up some meat, but it would have to do.

It was tough and stringy and didn't taste like much, but Tom and Lanny ate some of it anyway. It felt good to sit close to the fire and feel the heat burn the dampness out of their bones. The Apache woman and boy had walked away from them and gone down to the river. To look again for signs, they supposed, but it looked like there'd be none.

"We ought to've brought along some beans," Lanny said.

"Hindsight don't help much.

"I may start watching for circling buzzards pretty soon."

"I reckon a little carrion would taste as good as this." Tom felt tired and sleepy and wished they could get this over with. He worked on a bite of jackrabbit and got it down, then stretched out in the grass, put his head back and dozed.

Sage lay wrapped in their blankets asleep or knocked out by the fever that seemed to get hotter by the hour. Lanny walked over to the man, still chewing a mouthful of the stringy meat.

"You know how to amputate a leg, Tom?"

The question brought him out of his half-sleep. "Is it coming to that, you think?"

"Don't know. It'd be up to the other two, anyway, and I doubt they'd say get out the knife."

"The man's a danged Apache brave, Lanny. He wouldn't say it either." Tom saw the mother and son walking back from the river. From a cord in her hand hung two blue catfish. He nodded their direction and Lanny looked around and smiled.

"I suspect we need to build up that fire a little bit."

CHAPTER 31

The argument took longer and got hotter when they were ready to ride again. Finally the woman turned her back on them and would say nothing else.

Tom said, "You think we'll have to drag her back?"

"That's the case, near as I can tell. She intends finding her girl, dead or alive."

She stood with her eyes closed and her back stiff, breath coming deep and fast. Tom knew she was grieving, but it didn't make any sense to keep going downriver with a dying man and no provisions. He looked at Lanny and got back a shrug of shoulders. The country around them was quiet the way it can get in the middle of the day, the scent of damp ground rising and the slap of water from the river. In the mix of that, the tail end of loud conversation floated to them from a distance.

The two men turned to watch that direction and after a minute saw riders coming; four of them abreast, aiming straight ahead. Two figures walked behind them. Tom heard a shout from the boy and both Apaches broke into a run toward the group.

"Looks like the lost have been found," Lanny said. He walked to the horses and came back carrying two rifles. He put the Henry in Tom's hands. "Won't hurt to keep that handy."

The riders were cowhands by appearance, in good humor, wearing smiles. One of them held the end of a lariat looped around his saddle horn, trailing behind his horse and knotted to the waists of two Apache women that Tom recognized. Sage's wife clung to the arm of the younger one. The boy walked a few paces behind his sister trying to keep joy off his face. Both women looked like they'd been nearly beaten to death by the river or rough treatment or both. Their clothing barely hung on their bodies, mud-soaked and streaked and he could read exhaustion in their movements while the horse pulled them ahead.

"Looks like we captured the whole tribe," the lead rider said, pulling up beside Tom.

Nobody he recognized. The daughter caught sight of Sage where he lay and tried to run to him, but a yank on the lariat stopped her short and threw her down. She struggled to get back on her feet. Lanny walked over and took her hand. He lifted her up and helped her straighten her clothes while he said some things to her in a low voice.

The second woman, the one Tom figured was the wife of that other Indian, Yellow Bow or whatever they called him, kept her eyes on the ground. Besides the mud and the rough treatment, she was in great distress, crying out in sharp barks of pain.

"Not much of a tribe, I reckon," Tom said. "Just some folks caught in a bad spot."

"We'll take these off your hands. Headed over to the Loup place. Phil's a militiaman, and he'll know what to do with 'em."

None of the riders wore pistols, but every saddle carried a long gun. Tom said, "I'd offer you coffee but we just broke camp." He didn't like looking up at the man and stepped back a little. He wished they'd all dismount. It would make it easier to talk, but they stayed seated and acted like they expected to take all the Apaches with them. He went on, "No, sir, I can't turn this hurt man over to you. He's liable to die from that leg if we don't get him some help. The rest of them's family and they ought to stay together. I know for a fact that Phil Loup quit the militia a while back, and besides that, the militia turned these people over to me. I'm watching out for them." He took another step back and said, "So what I want you to do is let the women loose. We'll take care of 'em."

The riders looked around at each other, not quite believing what they'd just heard. The smiles got bigger. The man in front of him said, "You must've been eatin' some of that peyote your red friends like so much." He swung off his horse and dropped

126

the reins to the ground. He was a tall man, like Tom, and well-built with skin that looked as thick and tough as steer hide behind a week of beard. He lifted his wide-brimmed hat off and dropped it on the ground next to the reins. He took three steps forward and came at Tom with a wide looping right hand.

Not much different from a thousand matches Tom had fought. The stranger put his whole body into it, like he'd probably done many a time in many a saloon. Tom saw it coming and shifted the Henry into his left hand and slid his weight over onto his left leg. The big cowboy's laughing face turned confused when his fist hit nothing but empty space, then contorted with pain when the peyote eater buried his fist in an unprotected stomach. The tall man bent, sucking wind and fighting for nothing now except his next breath. A thin, brown liquid, maybe his last cup of coffee, poured down from his mouth and he choked on it, coughing and struggling to breathe.

Tom considered another right fist into the man's face, but it was a cruelty he thought unnecessary. The other three riders made no move. Lanny held his own Winchester at port arms. Tom glanced across them and said "Anybody else?" Silence. He nodded at Lanny, who untied the women and tossed the loose rope aside.

To the man in front of him who was still working at breathing and getting it back a little at a time, Tom said, "You'll be all right in a minute, mister. You can pick up your hat and remount and lead these others somewhere else. Or, we can finish what you started." He waited for a response and got none. "But you can't whip me, and I'll hurt you if it goes on any longer. Understand me?"

A silent nod of the head and a deep intake of air and the man stood upright, went over to his hat, picked it up and put it back on, then threaded a foot into his stirrup. He hung there just like that for a few seconds, like he might change his mind, looked back at Tom and nodded his head again and got aboard. The other three followed him as they walked their horses upriver, one of them coiling the lariat he'd used to pull the two helpless women through the thorns of the morning.

Tom and Lanny got the fevered Apache onto his feet and half-carried him to the Apaloosa mare. When they lifted him up he cried out from the pain, something he would never have done had he been awake. Tom said, "You think she can keep him in the saddle?" He'd made up his mind they had to go back. No more aimless travel.

Lanny thought about it. "I think we better tie him up there if we expect to keep him in one piece. He'll fall over for sure we don't." The boy stood watching his mother and the other two women talking, telling their stories to each other.

"They're saying the other Indian and his little boy, they're gone, drowned in the river. Horses, gear, everything washed away. These poor folks is destitute, Tom."

"Wish we had another horse. Two of us will be afoot no matter how we slice the cake."

Lanny's eyes shifted. Tom turned to see the riders coming back at a slow trot. He sighed and felt the weariness settling in his shoulders again. "Changed their mind. I guess."

CHAPTER 32

But it wasn't fight the others came back for.

"We talked it over, and however you look at it, we was wrong and I want to say I'm sorry I took that swing at you."

The stranger had his hat off, resting it on his leg. There was shame on his face, but Tom didn't trust it and kept himself ready if this was about to turn rough again. None of them had gotten down off their mounts. "Okay by me, then. No hard feelings."

"We know a place you might get some help for that there brave."

"What? A doctor? Out here?"

"No, but there's a mission across the river a few miles south. Out in the middle of nowhere, but the padre there is a doctor of sorts. He'd know what to do, anyway."

"Well, much obliged, but I think we better head home. No way for all of us to travel."

"We can help you. Ride a couple of you double, get you all to the mission."

Tom turned to Lanny. "What do you think?"

"Plain to me, Tom. These is angels in disguise."

The mission was just as the cowboy had described, in the middle of nowhere after a ride that took them past daylight into the early part of night. It was laid out beside a stream of water that reminded Tom of his own creek. And there were lights in windows, something unexpected and warm in the midst of indifferent darkness. The mission itself was made of limestone that shone in the night, and scattered around it were adobe huts, half a dozen or more, and in most of them the flickering light of a candle.

Their presence brought three robed men who admitted them to the little chapel, then helped carry the injured Apache into a tiny room and onto a narrow bed. Another one came then, another priest, or monk, or whatever they called themselves. And Tom told him what had happened, watching the steady eyes looking back with concern and care. Knowing they'd found a good destination, all right. Knowing they'd come to a place of healing.

Their angels in disguise, as Lanny had called them, shook hands all around and seemed relieved to have it done. They left soon after, saying a night ride was nothing to them, knowing the country well and wanting to get away from this embarrassment. The robes put out food for them all, on a plank table behind the chapel, but the cowboys were anxious to be gone and it was left to Tom and Lanny and the Indians. Beans and hominy and cold cornbread. Creek water for a drink.

"Tastes like manna from heaven," Lanny offered between bites.

The man in charge thought he could save their hurt Indian. "You did a good job with the break. Nearly as I can tell, the bone is in place, but there's a lot of swelling."

Tom said, "We thought gangrene might set in."

"Still might, of course, but I'll do what I can. I'm Father William."

Sleeping arrangements were made for the women and boy. Tom and Lanny got their bedrolls back and made do behind the altar in the chapel. There was a carpet on the floor there, though who knew how that had come about. Lanny found an old tin can somewhere for a spit cup and brought it with him, fixed a wad of snuff under his lip and rolled up inside his blanket.

Tom noticed a spicy smell around them. Candles, waiting to be lit. They both slept well, all the way to morning.

Almost morning, anyway. Before daylight a half dozen holy men in long habits with the hoods laid back, most heads bald or near to it, came into the chapel carrying burning candles and sat down on benches that served as pews.

It was a silent start to the day, but enough commotion to wake the two men up. Day didn't begin with coffee here, but after the prayers and a short talk by their leader, to which Tom and Lanny paid little attention, it broke up and there was more cornbread and creek water for breakfast.

Father William found them while they were saddling up. "That's a fine looking black," he said.

"He's a good one, all right. A bit of trouble, though. We left him penned up at home, but he broke out and followed us. No telling what I'll find when we get back."

"A stallion can be hard to handle." He laughed. "I did my share of it, too, back in Kentucky."

"Worked with horses?" Lanny said.

"Oh, yes, many years. Before I took vows, of course, and came here."

"We heard you was a doctor."

He laughed again, not a big man, but healthy looking and strong, a tanned face that said he spent his time outside, a full head of gray hair parted down the middle. "I was a veterinarian. I doctored horses. Long time ago."

Something moved across the smile on his face, sadness or pain. Then it was gone and he said, "I do what I can for the people when it's called for, like now, but no, I don't fancy myself a doctor. I'm a farmer and raiser of a few cows and sheep. And a saver of souls, I pray."

Tom finished buckling the cinch on the mare and said, "I met some people a while back came up to my place. Mexicans, good people. There was a girl said she learned to talk English at a mission school. I was wondering if maybe this is the place."

The priest thought a moment. "Could be, I suppose. We have some classes in language now and then. Latin, a bit of English. Children come, but I don't know who the child would be, the one you mention."

"It was a whole family. I was sick. They'd come up to gather pecans and they nursed me and got me back on my feet again.

Well, the old woman did. She's a curandera, got a little old dried up snakeskin supposed to be magic."

"You don't know their name?"

"No, seems strange now that I don't, but they didn't volunteer much, either. They acted a little scared to be there."

"North of the Loup range?"

It surprised Tom that the man knew about Loup. "Why, yes, that's right."

"The homestead of the young German. The one who died in that dark time."

"Yes, I own it now."

"I know about the trouble there; know it well. You've put yourself in the middle of a bloody feud."

"Looks like it, but no matter. I aim to stay."

Father William turned his head away from Tom's steady gaze, watched three men in heavy garments walk past carrying long-handled hoes. He breathed deep and let it out and said, "I'd better get back to the Indian. He needs looking after. If you need help you can always come here. Will you remember that?"

"I will. And much obliged."

"Now I'll surprise you a little more. I know the old woman you spoke of. She comes here often, and she helps me when we have sick people. Sometime today I will send for her again. The people you brought last night have need of her."

132

CHAPTER 33

When they forded the river, picking their way through the piles of drift, and climbed up to level ground again Lanny spoke up. "I vote we stop here and cook up some coffee. I can't go much longer without it."

"Sounds about right to me."

They left the saddles on, but slipped the bridle bits out of their horses' mouths and let them graze beside the black who was already after his share of grass. The bickering between him and Lanny's gelding had simmered down and it appeared they'd made a truce in their little war.

Tom drank half his brew in one long swallow, ignoring the heat of it, and leaned back against a liveoak sapling. The sun was halfway up the sky and the small tree cast a shadow across their coals. He picked up the pot and refilled his cup. "I'll be glad to get home again."

It was a long ride, but the ground had about dried out, footing was good and they made it before dark. There was enough light to see the damage to his horse pen. Though not as bad as Tom had expected, it was bad enough. The night turned cold. Tom carried in some wood and built a fire. They had biscuits and jerky for supper and slept that night the way exhausted men do.

At the little mission they'd left behind that morning the Apache, Sage, no longer burned with fever. His wife had held him upright while the old Mexican caused him to drink from the bottle she had brought with her. Now the healer woman sat in a chair in the corner of the room, wrapped in one of the blankets Father had given them. The others had bathed in the creek and wore clothing that the catholic men had provided, men's clothes, but clean and concealing. They sat or stood, all of them watching the man breathe in deep and normal rhythm. In another of the tiny rooms the boy slept alone.

"I need some smooth wire for that pen." They'd been up since daylight, made a meal on coffee and cold biscuits from last night and looked closer at the holes where his black had kicked his way out. "That rawhide is old and rotten. Needs replacing."

"Closest place would be up at Mason, don't you think?"

"I guess so, though I hate another trip just now. You could stay here and rest. I know you could use it."

"No, I'd just get lonesome thinkin' about you in the city havin' fun. I'd prefer to come along, you don't mind."

"We can bring back some civilized grub while we're at it. Live in style."

Lanny was looking at the little cabin. "When we come back and get the pen fixed I'd like to help you get the ceiling on your mansion plugged, too. We need to keep the weather outside."

Tom felt a sense of warmth from his friend that had been missing from his life for a while. "I'm sure glad you showed up, Lanny. I'm glad you're alive."

The Schneider place was on the way and Tom thought it was a good idea to stop off and tell them about the Indian scare that wasn't much of a scare. And, too, he liked the old woman. Her house, her operation, the land around her, felt like an anchor to him. Something solid and constant in his shifting life. Halfway there they saw smoke rising on the other side of a cedar brake.

Lanny said, "Somebody roastin' a sheep, I imagine." They rode through the cedars and found three men, one of them Ward Dobbins, at work in a wire pen full of the wooly four-footers that Lanny didn't care for. The fire smouldered under a big pot that gave off the smell of coffee.

Dust rose up where the men worked, the animals inside panicked, bleating and running in circles. One of them caught a lamb and carried it to where Dobbins stood waiting. The lamb was small, but you could see it was hard to hold onto. Sweat ran down the man's face and cut tiny rivers into the dust that covered him. His clothes had been dirty a while back, but were long past that, now. He got hold of the hind legs and lifted the little animal and Dobbins docked the tail and smeared something on it and the catcher let it go. It ran complaining to its mother.

The big foreman called out a greeting to Tom but stayed where he was while the other worker presented him with a fresh lamb. Lanny said, "I believe there's a wait involved if you want to talk to that feller. That coffee smells bad, but I've probably had worse."

Tom declined coffee, but got his pipe out of the saddlebag. The horses stood with their heads down, resting, the stallion on his lead rope raising an inquiring eye from time to time at the fuss inside the sheep pen.

The bowl of tobacco was half burned down when Dobbins called out to his helpers. "You men hold up and let's take a few minutes of rest. Get you some of that coffee if you want it. I need to go say howdy to our visitors."

His sleeves were rolled up and he had purple smears on his hands and forearms. He smelled like worm medicine. "Let's pass on a handshake," he said to Lanny when Tom introduced his friend.

Lanny said, "I thought this coffee had a familiar taste, and I realize now what it is. Guess I don't have to worry about parasites now."

"One of the benefits of working here, young fellow." He turned to Tom. "You look like you got your health back."

Tom told him about his visit to the Weiss farm.

"I've heard the story already from some visitors at headquarters. There was some depredation other places, though. Not much damage and no loss of life. Just a few braves sowing their wild oats, sounds like."

"I thought we'd stop off and pay respects to miz Schneider if she's home."

"No doubt she's there. That pretty Weiss girl and her brother are the visitors I mentioned. They came to stay a couple of days."

The lurch in Tom's chest felt like fear, but it wasn't the shameful fear he once felt. No, this was somethng else. Fear of the girl? Fear of his own foolishness? Whatever you called it, he knew something all at once that nobody had to tell him, something he had never dared hope for—she had come to find him.

CHAPTER 34

A two-horse buggy sat beside the house, its tongue on the ground, waiting to take the brother and sister back home, Tom figured. A sort of bonnet rose up over the seat, protection from sun and rain. He thought of how she would look riding in it, her skirt held out of the weather under the covering, trim and lovely, looking out at the countryside passing by. His throat ached.

He noticed the stain that would always mark this porch, the splintered board that would never be replaced. He thought of the Loups and their ways and the pigging string in his shirt pocket. He knocked on the door.

Tobias opened it, smiled when he recognized Tom, stepped back and motioned them inside.

Both men stood hats in hand in the neat parlor, the Schneider woman walking through her kitchen and Maria sitting in one of the chairs. She looked up with no expression on her face, neither gladness or distaste that he was there. She nodded hello to them and looked down at her lap.

The ranchwoman said, "We were talking about you this morning. You must've heard us."

Tom's throat was tight and he didn't trust himself to answer, but had to. Hadn't he left this awkward business behind on the road back from their farm? Tobias spoke up and saved him from the effort for a few seconds.

"We wanted to visit, but didn't know how to find you."

Tea was steeping in a china pot, the scent of it mingling with a tinge of woodsmoke from her stove, spreading through the house like perfume. "Let's sit down at the table and I'll give you each a nice cup of my strong tea." She was already putting out cups and Maria got up to help. Lanny stepped back outside,

137

spit out his snuff and came back in. They sat down and sipped at the tea. It was near boiling hot. The conversation took up where Tom had adopted his Apaches. Maria remained quiet, but the story excited Tobias.

"And the young boy, he swam it and brought back his papa?"

Tom nodded, and Lanny answered, "That's what the woman told me."

The Schneider woman said, "I have been to the mission."

"Yes, Ma'am," Tom said, "I figured you had. That priest talked like he knew about things around here. I thought maybe you was catholic yourself."

"Oh, no. A good German Lutheran is what I am. But, you know, when Mister Schneider died..." She paused. "When he, I should say, was murdered by that wolf, I questioned God. I questioned my own life. I cared for nothing. I went there searching, asking, hoping to find a way, a reason, to go on living." She stopped and drank a sup of tea, put down the cup and said, "I had not eaten food for over a week. They fed me and made me eat it, prayed with me, over me, for me, called back my soul, I think, from the dark place it had gone. So yes, he knows me, he knows of the hatred, the battle we fight here every day."

Tobias said, "I would swim the river to save papa." He gave them all a shy smile and dropped his head and scooted back in his chair, the matter settled.

Maria looked at Tom and said, "Since you left in the middle of the night we didn't get to thank you properly for your help."

He didn't know what to answer and so watched the cup in front of him, wishing this would end, wishing for sure they'd never come. Being close to her again was confusing and the knot in his stomach was growing.

The old woman smiled again, as if she understood something and said, "I was getting ready when you showed up to feed my chickens. Maria knows where I keep the feed. You two go and do it while the rest of us finish our tea, which is very good if I do say so. She looked at Tom, and he felt himself stand up and start for the door. The girl was slower, and for a second or two it appeared she wasn't coming. She sighed, moved her chair back from the table and followed.

It was a mixed flock of birds—white leghorns, a few of the banties that always remnded him of Lanny, and some red ones, bigger than the others. Two or three battalions of tiny chicks ran peeping after mother hens. A giant rooster, dark red, with some black and yellow streaks in his feathers, strutted unconcerned. All of it inside a pen of chicken wire. The wire ran to the sides of a wood shed, open in front with nestboxes in the back.

Maria led him behind the shed. "In this barrel," she said, lifting off the lid. She put it on the ground. The barrel was full almost to the top with some sort of small grain he didn't recognize. Milo, maybe. He liked the smell of it, thought of smells just like it back home. Well, back where home once was. A hoe and shovel leaned against the shed beside the barrel. The stink of manure hung in the air. She picked up a bucket and dipped it half full of the grain.

He took it from her and went back to the wire and threw it into the pen by the handful. The hens clucked and flew into each other and pecked the ground. They could probably use another half bucket, he thought, and refilled it while Maria watched. When he was done he saw that she had put the top on the barrel and seemed ready to go back inside. They hadn't talked at all, which was of course why the old woman had sent them out.

All at once the tightness in his throat and the knot in his belly went up in smoke and something else took their place. The heck with her, anyway. He didn't like the treatment she was handing out. "You act like I done something wrong. You come to thank me, you said, and now you got nothin' to say. I can't figure it out." He put the bucket down and waited. She looked at her feet and at the sky, took a step to go past him and stopped.

"I noticed how you looked at me the first time we met." Her eyes were brown with streaks of gold in them. They seemed to Tom to shine like the small stones you saw in creeks and rivers, tumbled and shaped by movement, magnified by the liquid stream."Then you came to our house and it was the same. I liked it." She met his sudden smile with her own. "I wanted to know you better."

He reached for her hand and she let him keep it. "You said you wasn't free."

"I am not promised, but my father makes his wishes clear."

"This Kirk fellow, I heard you might marry him."

"I might. He's asked and no one else has. He is German, like me, and it is what my father wants me to do."

No one else has. Was that an invitation? He couldn't let it pass. "If things worked out right for me, if I give it time and get to know you...I mean, maybe this is crazy, but would you ever consider marrying me?"

It didn't seem to surprise her. "My father would not like it."

"Well, I didn't put the question to him. I directed it at you."

She squeezed his hand. "It is an honor to be asked by you, but I don't feel free to say yes. It's different with my family. There is obligation. Alex Kirk expects it."

She walked away from him toward the house. He caught up and took her by the elbow. "Wait. This is important to me. I need some plain talk from you, not riddles and maybes, which is all I've heard."

The look on her face was almost anger, but not quite. "All right. Here is my plain talk. I wanted to see your face again and hear your voice. I wanted to get my heart and my mind still so I can decide things. And it is not so simple as you think. It is not about you, not *all* about you I should say." He liked the way she talked. Educated speech, slight Spanish accent. Spanish? Of course; she'd lived in Mexico for years. He remembered the first time they'd met and how Florian Weiss had said she and Tobias didn't speak good English. Must've been a joke, because she sure did.

"Kirk has asked me to marry him, yes, more than once. And I have not told him no. I have said I'll think about it, and I am. He's a good man, a handsome man. I like him very much when he is not silly, the way he was with his horse racing and his fists."

Tom said, "Well, I'm convinced. Maybe you should take him up on it." He'd heard all he wanted about Kirk. Sudden tears in her eyes made him sorry he'd said it.

"Now there is you."

"I don't want to make you cry." Before he knew it he had put his arms around her and pulled her close. He felt wetness on his shoulder through the cloth of his shirt. He smelled the clean scent of her, soap and rain and sun. A feeling came over him so intense it made him light-headed.

"Now there is you, and when I saw you ride your black horse and win that race and when I saw you turn your back when Kirk was jealous and tried to fight, you pierced me." She drew back and looked up at him. "You understand? Is this the plain talk you wanted?" He didn't answer. "You pierced me. Like a knife, a saber in the heart. Like what I never felt before. That is what you did."

He could think of nothing else to say except, "I'm sorry."

She laughed then, not a sad or cynical laugh, but a real one, and wiped the tears out of her eyes with the sleeves of her blouse. "You apologize? For being yourself? A bolt of lightning out of the sky? You are sorry I dream of you at night?"

Enough words. He kissed her, tasted her tears, felt her lips respond and believed in that moment that all things were possible, and that heaven had given him all he could ever ask for, "I'll come visit you," he said, I'll talk to your pa, explain myself to him. I'll court you as long as you need, whatever you want."

"You must not visit me. Not yet. Or talk to my papa. Give me time to think. I can not think if I am looking at you. There is more of the plain talk you asked for. Now I feel selfish that I have made you believe what I may not be able to do."

"What in thunder am I supposed to do, then?"

"I feel selfish again, but I ask you to wait. Let me have more time to think."

CHAPTER 35

The two found the road leading north and made the rest of their trip in near silence. Lanny tried, but Tom had little to say, wrapped up in his own thoughts. It was clear something had happened when the girl and his friend went outside to feed the chickens, which was nothing but an excuse for them be alone, anyhow. When they'd left and shut the door the little German lady had sighed and smiled and said, "Young love." After that they had talked about the weather til the couple came back.

They bought cans of food and a new supply of dry pintos, some lard and sugar. Coffee beans, some baking powder, a sack of flour. Two water buckets. Cartridges for their guns. A hammer and saw. A single-bitted axe. A pair of pliers. A wire cutter. Lanny said, "Much more we'll founder the horses."

"Just the wire is all."

When the clerk led them to the back of the store Tom found a roll of the smooth wire he wanted and said, "Believe I can use a couple rolls of chicken wire, too, if you got it."

They loaded their cargo on the Apaloosa mare. Lanny finished tying on the two rolls of chicken wire and said, "This poultry wire make you feel romantic?"

Tom laughed. "Let's stop off at the post office. I been thinking my mama might send a letter."

And he was right. A thick one, too, full of news that he read leaning against the hitch rail outside. Lanny had just remembered snuff, something that had slipped his mind during the buying spree, and was riding his gelding back to the store after it.

My Dear Son,

The first and most important thing I want to tell you is you don't have to worry about what happened in St. Louis. The man did not die.

He felt a weight lift off him with those words. He read them again and wanted to dance a jig. But how did she know?

We were surprised and taken aback by your letter, the things you told us, and most of all worried about your well-being in a hostile world. Well, you know your father. He is a determined man, and what he determined was to go himself, in person, to that city and find out the truth about what happened. Find out what, if anything, we could do for you.

He rode to Memphis and left his horse in a stable there. You will remember Blaze, his saddle horse, that gray dappled one with the white streak down his face. Well, he is still alive and healthy. Proof of his health is that he carried your father to Memphis and back with no trouble at all, old as he is.

Your father took a riverboat to St. Louis and just went to the police and asked about the incident you described. They had no record of it! No information at all. Well, to make a long story short, he kept on asking around the city, in Saloons and what have you, and at length some gambling types, men of low degree no doubt, remembered.

In your letter you said he was not breathing when you saw him last and a young lady was kneeling over him crying. A scene of great sorrow. But the witnesses your father found told him that after you had gone the man began breathing again, although he did not regain consciousness. Someone ran to tell you, but the boat had gone. As I suppose you know already, your opponent's name was Patrick O'Keefe. We call him Pat, and I'll tell you about that in a few more lines. He is a widower. The young woman you mentioned was his daughter, Suzanne. A beautiful and gracious young lady. I wish you would come home so you could meet her.

144

Yes, they are here at the farm. And how is that, you ask. Well, your determined father kept on asking and found the hospital where the fallen boxer had been carried, and found the very doctor who had saved his life. It was a stroke, you see. A clot or something like that in his brain that cut off the blood. One of the blows from your fists was the final cause, probably, but Suzy says he'd been having trouble for a long time, fainting spells and the like, and she'd begged him to stop fighting. He would not. They had fallen on hard times and needed the money he always said, and that's how it all happened.

You can see it was not your fault, son. He brought his condition into the fight with you and all of us think of you as a victim of foolishness, not a villain. And, if the incident has caused you to stop that loathsome fighting, then I consider it a gift from God.

Finally your father found their home, a boarding house, really. Pat had and still has difficulty walking. He has trouble with his left arm and leg. She was working in a store selling women's clothing to support them.

Your father says it took two days of persuasion before they agreed to come back with him. You know we're not rich folk, and all that travel was costly, but he felt obligated to help them if he could, and I am in agreement with him.

So they came to the farm, and here they live now. For a while, anyhow. Until Pat is better, at least. He walks about, helps your father as much as he can, and besides her cheerful company Suzy is such a help to me in the house and with my chores that I can hardly bear to think she will someday leave.

Has this letter lifted a cloud off you, darling son? I'll wager it has. Your father sends his good wishes and joins me in urging you to come home for a visit. We are hungry for the sight of you.

Tom could hardly believe it. He read the letter again, almost tasting the words. He folded it at last and slipped it into his pocket. He climbed into the saddle and headed the direction Lanny had gone, met him coming back and they stood their horses there, head to head in the dirt street while he told about the letter.

"That may be the best letter you ever get."

Tom laughed. "You find your snuff?"

"Oh, yeah. And I bought some nails while I was at it. We forgot, and a hammer ain't much use without some nails to hit."

"Well, there's still one more trip anyway. I need a tablet and pencil. I want to write back and get it sent while we're here."

No more than half an hour later the letter, just one sheet, but full of gratitude and promises he'd try to keep, was on its way and the two riders had cleared the last of the town. Tom said, "We've used up the day. You want to open up a can of beans and spend the night on the trail?"

"We could shoot us another jackrabbit." The comment got no response. "I figured you wanted to go back by Schneider's."

"Well, I do and I don't. I don't know where I stand with Maria, and the more we talk the less I know."

"Ain't that the way it always is?" Lanny broke out the new box of snuff and got the top off. He shoved it in a rear pocket when he was finished loading his lip. Tom smelled the musty sting of tobacco.

"Can't answer that. I never been in this situation before."

"Pretty gal." A bird flew out of a bush beside the narrow road and all three horses shied away from the sound. It was near dusk. The scent of cedar was strong. Lanny looked over at Tom. "If you want to save yourself from bewilderment, I vote we just ride on home, then."

"I thought I'd try buying some chicks from miz Schneider. Fried eggs for breakfast would be a good thing, don't you think?"

"I do, and there's the mystery of the chicken wire solved."

"Be better I guess to build the pen first and go back for the chicks another time."

"Better for the chickens. Disappointment for the coons and possums. And a whole lot less bewilderment for you."

A half-moon hung in a clear sky and lit the way. They found the big oak that was his turning place and kept on south. Tom got his pipe going and thought about the dark-eyed girl who'd stolen his heart. He wondered what he could do about her, how he should court her. It was too much for him, and he forced his thoughts into other paths. By the time they noticed the lighter sky in the far distance their conversation had run down and they were both feeling stiff and tired from the long ride.

"Looks like something burning down yonder," Lanny said. "What's out there?"

"Nothin' I remember." But that was not true. He already knew what it was, though he didn't want to say it or even think it. Not now, when things had seemed so good, when his life seemed like it was about to get back to the way he wanted it.

CHAPTER 36

They rode up on it with care, circled around it in the dark to be sure nobody else was watching. Heat still radiated off the coals, and that was all that was left of the cabin. Lanny said, "I smell coal oil." So did Tom. The burners had used a lot of it, wanted to make sure this time.

"You know who did it?"

"Not a doubt in my mind." He was tired. A whipporwill sang its night song somewhere among the trees, like all of this never happened. Just as if evil was not present in the world.

They had their bedrolls, they had weapons and ammunition. They had food and coffee and a creek full of water. And horse feed. And the pigging string was still in his shirt pocket. The raid must have come after dark, and why not? That's when evil does its work most of the time. Nobody had molested the feed or what was left of his pen. They didn't talk about it. No point. Just made camp out in the trees away from the smoke and dozed through a restless night, keeping the horses close and rifles in reach.

Morning was a surprise. Tom felt...happy? Not how he'd expected, anyhow. The cabin was gone, and the things inside it burned up or ruined. But O'keefe was alive in Tennessee, Lanny Tarver was alive six feet away, and maybe Maria was his to love. The trees were growing their pecans on land that belonged to him. The war, the feud he'd expected, had been declared. The whipporwill had gone quiet, and the squirrels had started their chatter.

The cabin's ashes were still hot, and would stay that way another day. Tom said, "It'll be a while before we can rake through 'em and see if anything survived." The flames had been

149

tall enough to reach up into the trees close by. Leaves had been burned away or shrivled into dry twists where they hung. Limbs charred. Tom found the old pecan tree he'd secreted all his papers in. Sometime in the past hundred years a woodpecker must've found a hole in the trunk, excavated it more and raised a few generations in it, then squirrels had used it for a warehouse til Tom found it and emptied it out to make room for the leather pouch. The tree leaned in such a way that falling rain passed it by.

Lanny carried his cup of coffee around, looking at things and saying very little until Tom had put the pouch back.

"I thought you'd be cussin' up a storm by now. But no, you're walkin' around hummin' a tune. Don't misunderstand me—I'm happy if you're happy."

"I wasn't hummin' any tune."

"Well, it was a...an abstraction, you could say."

"Abstraction."

"I probably need some more sleep."

"We ain't got the time for it right now. Don't you think we ought to at least build a leanto in case another storm comes up?"

They got it done by the middle of the day, using cedar limbs for the frame and thatched a roof on it with smaller cedar limbs. The needles would turn brown and wash away in a while, but for now it would keep the rain out. "Better than what you had," Lanny said.

And the horse pen, that had once been a goat pen, was repaired and put back in use before dark. They replaced the cedar pickets that had some rot, or been kicked to pieces by the stallion, and they wove the smooth wire in and out, holding the pickets in place just the way rawhide had once done. The black and Lanny's gelding had made uneasy peace, and all three animals were inside now, sharing it. Tom looked it over and thought to himself, *better than new.*

The crocks were still usable, though their contents had burned to ashes. The iron cookpot, the one the Mexican family had found, looked all right once they got the ashes out of it and washed it clean, and his frying pan survived, too. His tin plates were warped but still usable. Most of the coals had gone out, helped along by buckets of creekwater. Tom used the mattock to scrape down to the ground, looking for anything the fire had spared. The mattock hit metal and there was the branding iron he'd leaned in a corner and forgotten about. A useless thing to have, he'd figured all along. You couldn't brand a pecan, and that was his stock. But the horses ought to be marked as his against theft. He just had not gotten around to it. Putting a brand on anything, any other living creature, was not something he would ever do lightly. *I put my brand on the left hip.* It was a simple brand, like he'd told the blacksmith that day. A half-circle; a rainbow. He washed the iron clean in the creek and left it in the sun to dry.

Lanny was slow to get his boots on next morning. "You look like you feel bad."

"Oh, I still ain't all healed up from the wound, you know. Too much ridin' lately, I guess." He unbuttoned his shirt and showed Tom where the bullet had hit high up his chest on the left side. There was a spot, looked like an open sore, still leaking blood. "I just now sprung this new leak," he said. "Probably all our construction projects is what done it. I think I'm gonna have to leave it to you for a day or two. Watch the squirrels and dip snuff while you do whatever it is you got planned."

The little man had never seemed to run out of energy before. Tom knew he was hurting. "I got nothing planned but more construction. You take it easy while I go lookin' for some big cedar. I want to chop some good-sized logs for the new house."

"Not a cabin this time?"

"I ain't sure about the difference, but if you want something to bring a new bride to, I think it needs to be a house, don't you?"

Most of the cedar in that country grew bushy, with thin limbs covered in needles. Scratchy and useless. It shaded out grass for stock and used up water out of the ground. The ranchers and farmers aroundabout considered it a pestilence come to take the space between oaks and elms that could be better used to graze cattle and horses. Even sheep. In places it grew so thick a horse couldn't penetrate it. A man couldn't walk through it without scratching up his hands and face and filling his nose with the smell of its oil.

But sometimes it didn't grow that way at all. Sometimes, in the right kind of spot, shaded, down low where there was water, where Spanish oak prospered and good soil piled up as it washed off the high limestone hills, it was a different kind of cedar.

Maybe it was an altogether different tree, but still it was cedar, and it would last years without rot. Out of the tall, heavy trunks you could cut logs and build a house or a barn. You could saw boards for a porch to hold your rocking chairs.

It was the kind of place where varmints made their homes, dug holes in the loamy dirt, slept there and raised their litters there. Water and solitude and cool summers. And that's the sort of place Tom found. It wasn't far from his homestead, in a narrow valley cut by a smaller stream that fed his creek. The stream came in from the north, and he figured it led into Schneider's range. Nobody would begrudge a few cedars, anyway.

He'd learned to use an axe long ago when he was just a boy in Tennessee, and he knew how to swing the single-bit. He left the mare on a rope in tall grass, took off his shirt, and spent the morning chopping. He was tired and hungry by the time the sun got overhead and it turned hot down in the little valley where he had worked. A couple dozen logs of about the same size were piled where he'd dragged them, bark still on, the way he'd leave it, but all the branches trimmed.

His hands were sticky with cedar sap. Bits of wood stuck to the sweat on his chest and face, and he could feel it in his hair, too. He washed in the stream but it didn't help much with the sap. He needed coal oil to cut it. He put his shirt back on, retrieved the horse and tied his lariat to the end of the top log. Pulling it behind him was slow work over the rocks and through the trees going back. He wondered if there was a better way. If so, it probably involved men and wagons, and he had neither one.

No sign of his friend when he got the single log where he wanted it. He unsaddled the mare and turned her in with the other two. Lanny was asleep under the leanto holding his Winchester like a baby with both arms.

In front of the leanto the little cowboy had built a rock fire ring. He'd cut two upright pieces with forks at the top and driven them into the ground on either side of the ring, then laid a crosspiece into the forks and hung the iron pot. A fire burned under it now and the smell of cooking beans surrounded the leanto. Tom was plenty hungry and they had no meat. Instead of going back for more logs in the afternoon, which he didn't want to do anyway, he decided he'd do some hunting.

He got some corn meal and decided he'd fry mush to go with the beans. The beans were well cooked already and smelled good. When the mush was done he found enough tools to eat it all with and woke Lanny up.

"Thanks for doing some cooking. Here's you a plate."

"Man, I was dead asleep. Good thing no hostiles attacked while you was gone."

"I left a pile of logs way on up the creek. Think I'll go shoot a deer before it gets dark. How you feel?"

"Better. I Just need a short vacation from being manly."

CHAPTER 37

He went on foot with the Henry. Stayed close to the creek. Not a cloud in the sky today and the sun was hot on his back. His muscles felt tired and loose from the morning of axe work. Plenty more of it to come, too, but when Lanny felt better he'd be some help with all that cutting and hauling. He was careful and quiet, moving from cover to cover, tree to tree, watching for movement, listening for the rattle of brush. He wondered what Maria was doing just now. Wondered what she was thinking.

And there they were.

Small herd. Three does. A pair of twin fawns and two singles alongside their mamas, and one young buck, a yearling. Just a couple of points, and small enough to carry to camp. Tom wouldn't have to go back for a horse.

One shot, back of the shoulder. Loud, his ears ringing from it, the other deer running, gone from sight in a second or two, him alone then, smelling the tang of burned powder, walking to the young buck, lifting his big knife out of its scabbard.

He left the innards for the buzzards and coyotes, washed his knife and hands in the creek and slung the carcass across his back, the weight on his shoulders, the fore and hind feet down either side of his chest, something to hold onto. The Henry he carried cradled across his arms.

No more than a hundred steps later the sound of gunfire. Somewhere ahead; two shots spaced a few seconds apart. He paused to listen. Not another sound except birds in the trees over his head. He leaned the Henry against a blackjack oak and slid the deer carcass to the ground, then lifted it into the same tree, hung it in the crotch of a limb. No sense leaving it out for a hungry coyote. He picked up the Henry and set off again.

The scent of wet ashes and stale smoke met him, a reminder of evil and the need for caution. He bent low behind a patch of agarita bushes, their spiked leaves about man-high, and worked around it until he could see the leanto. Nobody moving, no sounds. Was Lanny all right? Please let it be so. Then, from behind the rock stack Tom had laid up for protection, there the little man came. He was staring past the black pile of ash out into the open country to the south.

Tom stayed where he was. Kept his voice down, but loud enough to be heard. "Lanny? What's goin' on?"

As much as he disliked walking, Lanny went back for the deer with Tom and told him about it on the way. Two riders. He saw them when they were still far off, hoped they'd just go on somewhere else, but they did not. Instead, they came straight toward this place, and not knowing what their business was, or who they were, but figuring the worst, he'd gone behind the rocks.

"I called out. I said hold on right there, would you. They pulled up a second or two and then spurred right ahead like I hadn't said hold on."

"So you shot at 'em. Don't blame you a bit."

"Not *at* 'em. No, just in the air over their heads. First shot stopped 'em, but it took another one to invite their absence. Turned tail finally and went. What I figured was, it was the burners, or some of 'em, anyway."

"Well, I don't know for sure who it was, but I can guess. And I think they'll be back."

A few hours were left til dark and Tom decided to haul two or three more of the logs he'd cut that morning. Lanny stayed behind to dress out the buck. Pulling the logs was slow work and by the time he came back with the third one he decided to turn the mare loose and quit for the day. He'd managed some progress, and thought it was not a good idea to leave his friend alone for too long, feeling punk like he was and strangers coming around. He took a bath in the creek. The cold water felt good after a sweaty day. Walking back, he smelled frying meat.

They sat beside the leanto after supper, watching the day turn dim. Still not a cloud up there, and Tom thought it a good thing. No need to test their thatch job so soon. Birds came and went, up into the trees and down into the agarita bushes after the red berries. Mockingbirds seemed to get the best of it, screeching and threatening small ones, running them off only to have them sneak back from another direction. Kept everybody busy. And, here and there a bluejay dived in and scattered the whole bunch. Even the mockers gave way.

Lanny had his usual dip of snuff working, and Tom had lit his pipe. Danger was in the air, but a kind of contentment dulled its edges for Tom. He still felt just like he had when he woke up all those long hours ago. A buzz of happiness that didn't have to have a reason. It just was. And yet, under it all was an insistent need to strike back.

"You could sell admission to that bird show."Lanny spit in that direction. "I've been to a stage production down in San Antone. Pretty women, actors and all, and I think the birds have got it beat."

"How you comin' along?"

"Ways to go, I reckon, but the rest done me good today. You could say I'm perky."

"I don't know that I'd say that."

"I'm fine. You can say that."

"I want to ask a favor of you, Lanny."

It was nearly dark. Thin strips of venison hung on the crosspiece above low flames, drying out. Meat they could save for a day or two. The birds kept up their racket.

"Anything you want."

Tom drew on the pipe, blew smoke from the corner of his mouth, and said, "I want you to stay here again tomorrow."

"You need help pullin' all them logs in. I can do that, no trouble."

"Well, what I'm thinking is, the logs can stay put a day or two. I'm gonna make a short journey."

157

"Goin' after chickens? Pen ain't built. Goin' after that pretty gal?"

He shook the ashes out of his pipe and put it away. "Wasn't much of a cabin. Already half burned down."

Lanny kept his mouth shut and waited for the rest of it.

"I got a deed says it was mine, though."

"You can make a complaint to the county sheriff."

Tom shook his head. True night was about on them. The air had a new scent coming off the ground, the creek, the big trees. The birds had gone quiet. "Get no help there."

"You know who done it, though."

"No proof of it."

"But you know."

"I'm about to take a ride. I need you to stay here."

"I can't see no reason I can't go along. Why?"

"One is better than two this time, is all. I'm riding the black in case I get in a chase, and he'd leave Charley behind."

"Now listen..."

Tom put a hand on his friend's arm. "Stay here. Please. I'll be back."

CHAPTER 38

He knew the general direction of the Loup headquarters. Somewhere southeast. It couldn't be a very long ride, either. The father and son hadn't been far from home the day they'd come on him with their guns and threats and brandings. Tom felt the hard desire walk up his throat like a centipede, a desire he had kept quiet for a long time. A feeling he'd thought for a while he might put away forever. Not forgive it, but just leave it be. He couldn't name the feeling, had never felt such a thing in his whole life, even in wartime. He wanted to kill those people, those two who had done it to him. Wanted their blood on his hands, wanted to see them afraid, hear them beg, wanted to watch the light go out in their eyes.

But he wasn't after that tonight. It could wait. If he waited long enough, maybe he could wash it out of his system. Tonight was something else. Tonight he was a messenger, and the message was, *an eye for an eye.*

Far to the south he saw a blink of lightning fork from cloud to cloud. No thunder. Too far away. A small storm blowing up from the Gulf of Mexico. He kept the stallion at a slow walk. It was still dark out here, and though the big horse was fast he wasn't a cowpony and might put a foot in a rabbit hole he couldn't see. It wouldn't be long til there'd be some light from the coming dawn.

He'd slept a few hours, and sometime after midnight he had left the leanto and saddled the horse in the dark. There'd been no more talk. It had been a silent and lonesome leaving, but he'd told Lanny the truth. The gelding couldn't keep up if he had to run.

159

Another truth, the one he'd kept to himself, a truth stronger than the other one, was this: he didn't want to share with anybody what he rode to do. Wanted it silent and private.

He went on, with all of it boiling in him, and when dull light showed in the eastern sky the gulf storm had come a little closer. Stars went out and the hills smelled like morning, fresh and promising. It was a lie, but maybe mornings had to lie, else men might decide to hide from the days. He rode up a sharp rise through a stand of beebrush, their white flowers shaking loose and falling when the stallion pushed through. When they crested it, there below was what he'd come to find.

The main house and everything around it looked worn and old, like it had been there since the first day of the world. Like it had been sitting in its little valley forever. Maybe it had. The house was stone, fieldstone that may have started out white, but was turned shades of gray and brown and near-black from time and weather. Lucky for the Loups it wouldn't burn.

Near the house a long, low, tin-roofed something with a half-dozen men standing in front of it. Bunkhouse. Built of unpainted boards and batts like the cookshack beside it. Smoke drifted out of the shack's chimney. Behind the bunkhouse a taller structure, a barn, it's boards dark and warping, its tin roof long ago covered by rust. They'd been fed by now and he guessed they were about to rope horses out of the corral close by and spread out for work, or maybe burning somebody's property.

Tom stood down and tied his mount away from the crest of the hill. He came back where he could watch, sat down and leaned against a boulder that had rolled from somewhere higher a thousand years or a thousand days ago and looked like it might decide to go again.

Another half an hour went by while the figures below him cut out their horses from the remuda inside the corral fence, got them saddled and lasted out the bucking of a few. He remembered the crazy mare and the way she had always started the day. She'd been crazy, all right, and easy to hate, but like the cabin, she had been *his*. Clouds built on the southern horizon

160

and the lightning kept up its occasional flash. He heard a faint, faraway rumble of thunder. There'd be rain today. He thought about Lanny back there under the leanto and hoped the roof they'd put on it kept the water out.

Once they were mounted the ranch hands took out in different directions. Two men, each leading a saddled horse behind his own, rode together to the front of the house and sat there a few minutes until two others came out the door. That would be father and son, he thought, and the feeling he couldn't name came up into his throat again, tasting red and salty as blood. He tried to spit it out, but it stayed. The two men mounted their horses and the quartet rode away to the east, out of sight behind a stand of liveoaks.

Time to do it. He took the box of matches and the old canteen out of the saddlebag and climbed on the black racer. It took a minute to find a way down this side of the steep hill.

The smell of cooking still hung in the air. Fried pork, biscuits, coffee. The man or woman who'd done the cooking might still be around. In that shack beside the bunkhouse, probably. Maybe a housekeeper in the big limestone. He tasted the feeling again and let it grow, let it take hold of him. Behind the barn he found a corncrib and a smokehouse, both built of the same kind of logs he'd cut the day before, low enough that he hadn't seen them from the hilltop earlier. He opened the canteen and poured a clear liquid at the corner of each in turn and dropped a match on the spots. The wood was dry and quick to catch. He'd have to hurry. There'd be smoke in a couple of minutes.

Quick now. Not the barn. Maybe animals in there. The cook-shack caught like the others. He raced to the corral gate and swung it open, rode the black inside and drove the horses out. A man came out the front door of the shack, saw him and disappeared inside again.

Was it enough? The red, salty feeling turned black and filled him up, a rage he'd never felt pushed him toward the stone house that wouldn't burn. Inside were things that would, though. Inside, where the men lived. The two who killed and

161

burned, who beat and branded. Somebody yelled behind him, a rifle boomed and something yanked at the sleeve of his shirt. His arm burned. He pulled the Henry and swung around in the saddle, firing at the man's feet. A man he didn't know, didn't want to know, didn't want to kill. The man dropped his rifle and fell backward, tried to reach the weapon again. Tom fired at the log frame of the door and watched him crawl out of sight.

The house. Was there time? He didn't care. Time or not, he would burn their beds, the table they sat at, the chairs they rested on. The stallion took him to the door and he slid to the ground, canteen over his shoulder, the Henry in his left hand, the matchbox in his pocket.

A woman stood there. The entrance was recessed a couple of feet under the rock wall to make a narrow porch that extended halfway across. She stared at him. Not afraid, not threatening. Her left hand on the high back of a wooden rocker, her right hand at her throat. She was not old, not young, a plain woman with the rough skin of a working life. She wore a blue print dress and was barefoot. Her hair was dark, streaked with gray and twisted into a bun.

No housekeeper. It was her house. Her doorway she stood in front of. In his thoughts about the Loup men Tom had never considered a wife and mother. These were not the kind of men whose mornings and evenings were rounded off and smoothed by the presence of a woman. In his mind they were like the things he knew they'd done—stark, angry, murderous.

She made no effort to speak, just watched him and stood her ground. She would not let him through the door easy. He thought of his own mother. This woman couldn't be that kind, not living here and married to that man. But no matter. The darkness in him went gray. He poured out the canteen on the grass where he stood, cradled the Henry under his arm, struck another match and dropped it. Fire rose up. He felt its heat on his back as his boot found the stirrup again.

162

CHAPTER 39

Leaning over his saddlehorn, he let the black run. Two hundred yards away now and picking up speed. Somewhere behind, he heard the rifle again, but the bullet didn't reach him. He glanced back and saw two figures, one stamping out the fire he'd left in their yard, the other, in blue, standing still in the same place, watching him ride away.

The horses he'd turned out were scattered all around, nipping at the short, overgrazed grass of the valley. He urged the stallion through a pass that put him higher. The land leveled off. This was all new country to him, but home was northwest. He pulled the black down to a trot and looked around. Nobody. He circled cedar brakes and stands of mesquite. The mesquite trees carried a heavy crop of beans this summer. A crop that had once helped feed the native people of these hills. More thunder back south. He caught the scent of rain on a sudden wind. Smoke, too. He wondered if the rain would come soon enough to put out the fires he'd set. It didn't matter. Whatever harm the Loups brought him, he would carry it back. Now they knew it. That's what mattered.

He started to throw the empty canteen away, thought better of it and stuffed it along with the matchbox in a saddlebag. Couldn't tell, might need it again for one reason or another. Utensils of any kind were not easy come by out here. The bad feelings that had tormented him all night had burned out. He felt clean, felt light, like he could flap his arms and fly away. And hungry. That would have to wait.

Tom kept the stallion at a steady trot, figured the big horse could stay at it all day and it wouldn't tire him out in case speed was called for. He rolled up the ripped sleeve on his right arm. The rifle bullet had creased him was all, left a burnt trail across

163

the top of his arm maybe two inches long. Not deep, though, and there wasn't much blood. It would be sore for a week or two, but nothing to worry about. He rolled the sleeve back down and buttoned the cuff.

Three riders came out of a cedar brake off to his right and galloped straight at him.

He jerked the reins the other direction and planted his heels in the stallion's flanks. There was open country ahead. Bunches of cattle that had congregated over the best grass went running all directions. He looked over his shoulder. Still coming, but they hadn't gained on him Weapons glinted in their hands. They meant to shoot. Had he used up all his luck already this morning?

He'd bought the horse for times like this, and now he'd find out if the price had been worth it. Another glance back. They were losing distance on him. He wished he knew the country better, knew which way to go.

But he didn't, and that was the sorry truth. So he guessed. And a mile farther on he saw he'd guessed wrong.

He'd doubled the distance and the pursuers were far enough behind there wasn't much chance of a bullet in the back, though he heard the twang of a richochet now and then, off a tall oak, or off the side of one of the low cliffs sheared into the hills he dodged through. Then the cliffs raised up higher on both sides and the only way to run was straight ahead. The black was slowing down. He was fast, all right, could outrun anything around here for a mile or two, but a horse like this wasn't bred for the long haul. Not like a work-hardened cowpony, not like the wild mustangs of this country that could run all day without rest. A narrow stream of water shone ahead, with a high bank on the other side of it, running beside it and too high to climb. He'd be nothing but a target hanging up there anyway, if he tried it. Another bullet, close enough he heard it hum when it passed by. If he kept running, he was going to lose this horse; foundered or shot. Dead either way. He wouldn't allow it.

He rode into the creek and across it, water kicking high enough to wet his pants legs. It was on a shallow bed, over rock, and must have been running just like this since the earth was a baby, cutting its way down to here. A bullet clipped caliche out of the cliff face in front of Tom. Nowhere to go. He jerked the stallion to a stop, found the box of shells in one of the saddlebags and hit the ground with the reins in has hands, looking to find some kind of shelter for his big horse.

A few seconds more, watching for the riders to come into range, seeing one, then another, appear then disappear as they came down the same trail he'd followed, knowing he'd be trapped here. They came into the open pushing hard, leaning low, three abreast. He couldn't make out their faces at that distance, wouldn't know them, anyway, and like the man back at the cookshack, he didn't want to kill them. Not today, anyhow.

One of them pulled a length ahead of the others on a low-slung bay pony with two white feet. The left front and the right rear. Funny thing to pay attention to, Tom thought as he raised the Henry and dropped the bay head-first and rolling forward out from under the rider. Eye for eye. Horse for horse, though it felt like a sinful act.

The others fought their mounts to a hard stop and jumped to the ground to grab hold of the man who lay still beside the bay. They pulled him behind an offering of low mesquite that didn't provide much cover. The bay raised his head a time or two, like he was about to stand up. Tom knew he'd killed the animal and took no joy in it. He felt like he'd felt many a time in that futile war. *Them or me, so better them.*

A shot from the mesquites. Bits of caliche rained down. The other two horses started grazing on grass that grew beside the trail as if human craziness was not worth paying attention to. Tom could have killed both animals and left the men afoot. But no more death today, man or beast, if he had any say in the matter. He fired into the thorny trees, keeping it high, keeping their heads down. Nothing to do with the black but tie him to one of the sparse saplings that grew alongside the creek. No real cover, but the best he could manage.

Another horse then, another rider, just what he'd worried about most, coming fast, then reining up at sight of the grazers. There might be more coming. He'd cooked his own goose, all right. The stallion whinnied. The new horse whinnied back. Tom looked closer. Lanny?

CHAPTER 40

His friend saw him and raised an arm to let him know it, then wheeled around and disappeared from sight just as another rifle shot exploded out of the mesquites, aimed not at Tom this time, but at the little rooster. These people must carry a lot of ammunition. They'd wasted a bunch already. He knew Lanny well enough to understand it was a temporary retreat. He'd have to watch and wait and maybe they could get the two men out of their cover. Not apt to come at him on foot, and the horses cropped grass out in plain sight despite the iron bits in their mouths. It had turned into a standoff now. He moved closer to the stallion and crouched there, saw movement in the mesquites and put another shot above it, watched leaves scatter and fall.

No more shots. A few minutes passed and he wondered if they'd slipped away, or maybe decided to chase him down afoot. Where was Lanny? Right here, somewhere, that was sure. The creek made its sounds riffling over its shallow bed. A bird or two tried its song. He almost felt like he'd dreamed it all.

"Here we come, Tom! Don't shoot!"

Loud in the quiet. A drop of rain hit Tom's face, slanting in under the brim of his hat. The two men came walking with their hands over their heads and Lanny behind them.

Tom rode the stallion back across the creek. More rain fell. Thunder fussed somewhere south. "Good thing I disobeyed orders, General."

Nothing for it but to shake his head. "Plenty glad to see you, too." He got down and walked over to the group of men. "What about the other one?"

The two Loop riders kept their hands high and offered no answer. Lanny said, "He's back there restin'."

"Is he hurt bad?"

Lanny grinned. "I'd say he's nearly fine. All except for a couple of fingers that appears to be not as fine as they was. And some general confusion."

"See anybody else around here?"

"I think it's just us."

Both their prisoners stared at the ground, nothing to say. They were slender men in working clothes, browned by sun and weather. Maybe plain ranch hands and nothing to do with what had happened to his cabin. He said, "I'm sorry about the horse." They didn't seem to hear. "We'll lead your mounts up the trail a ways. You'll have to walk back up there to find 'em, but they'll be tied and waiting for you."

Lanny said, "We better gather up all the guns, too. Save these men from the bitter fruit of temptation."

The rain was coming harder by the time they got the two horses settled, and they wrapped up in their slickers for the ride still in front of them. Lanny said, "We seem to do a lot of ridin' in rainstorms." Their animals walked with heads down, careful where they stepped.

"Just so it's clear, I'm happy you came out here and found me, but I was surprised. Anything happen back home?"

"Is that what you call that leanto? Home?"

"Yeah. It's where the coffee's at. Somethin' happen?"

"You've heard of female intuition. Well, I had a dose of that without the female part. I was worried you'd get youself in over your head in a mess you couldn't get out of, and next thing I knew, me and Charley was off to the rescue. Heard all that shootin' and naturally gravitated to it."

"Good luck for me you did. Bad luck is, now there's three or four people can tell the law I'm the one done the burning and put down that poor horse."

"You might ought to leave this country for a while."

"No, I'll not be run off. It ain't your fight, though, and I'm the one put you in the same fix. Maybe you ought to ride back to the Bigboy now and stay out of my troubles."

The clouds blew past them and the rain let up. Patches of blue sky showed here and there. "You ain't said what mischief you pulled."

"I set fire to their corn crib and smokehouse, and a cookshack. Didn't stay to watch. Rain may've put it out for all I know. About the time I thought I was in the clear the three back there took to chasing me and ran me into that blind canyon."

"You said three or *four* people."

"Well...there was a woman. On the porch. Stared me down. Wife, I guess."

He remembered the look on her face. Hard to pin it down, but it had kept him from pushing his way inside her house, and he was glad of it now. By another hour the overhead sky had turned clear. Just a few clouds showing to the north. The sun felt like a hot hand pressing down on Tom's shoulders. The stallion's easy gait made it hard to stay awake. A short siesta was what he wanted. Maybe a long siesta.

The two horses began to chuckle deep in their throats when they neared the creek, talking to the appaloosa mare. Her head and neck stretched over the top of the cedar pickets. Her eyes were wide and white.

"You feed that gal anything? I sure didn't. Thought I'd be back before now."

Miles away, across the Pedernales river, outside the little mission, men in heavy dark habits hoed weeds in a field of beans. They sweated in silence, content with the work, the life they lived.

Inside, in one of the rooms behind the chapel, rooms kept for strangers who wandered here in need of help and healing, the Apache, Sage, lay sleeping still. He had come awake three times since the old curandera had arrived and each time she had given him her bitter water to drink. The boy sat on the floor with his back against a wall, his face vacant with waiting. The woman, his wife, stood beside the bed as she had stood through the last day and the night that followed. The other two had found a place to sleep, weary with loss and the bad fortune of this journey.

Sage wandered through hills and valleys he had never seen before. There were colors in the sky above. And where he walked, or dreamed he walked, the grass was thick and green under his feet. And soft. The air he breathed smelled of the blue flowers that always covered the hills in springtimes he had known. And there was no more pain in his leg. He would have liked riding his horse through this pretty country, but he remembered the horse had drowned in that high river. So he would walk, and the walking was all right. He didn't know which way to go, but also knew it didn't matter. Any direction at all would lead him back.

The father tapped his knuckles on the open door in courtesy and walked over to stand beside the wife. He reached down and touched the skin bracelet the old woman had fastened on the Indian's wrist. He shook his head and smiled. He had asked God's forgiveness many times in the past about this business of the old woman and her charms. The people responded to her, though. More than to his own prayers. They often got better. He had seen it happen. It was a part of their belief system, he had long ago decided, that would never be done away with while this generation lived. Time would change it, of course. For now, this man's fever had vanished and he rested with no cries of pain. Good enough.

The boy got up from the floor and went back to the tiny room he'd slept in and found his bow and the three blunt arrows. The string was dry now and would throw an arrow as it always had done. He walked outside into the sunshine and wandered down a deer trail beside the creek. It felt good to hold the weapon again. He thought of the many rabbits and squirrels he'd taken with it. He could bring one down now if it showed itself.

He remembered how afraid he'd been when he went after his father. How the current had taken him and then let him go free. How it had felt to pull Sage to safety. How it felt now to know at last the man would live.

170

CHAPTER 41

It was hard work. Two weeks of chopping cedar and snaking the logs over rocks and through mesquite, scrubbing off the sap with kerosene after supper. Tom did the axe work and Lanny the riding, swapping off his gelding and the appaloosa mare to save wear and tear on the animals.

They made their way to the cutting spot before daylight in the mornings while a touch of coolness still hung in the air. It was down to a routine by now. A fire for coffee first, then soon as he could see, Tom began working. Bringing a tree down was the quickest part. Trimming took longer. The smell of the wood, smoke from the fire and the oil from the needles thickened as the sun got higher.

Even on the days when his arms felt stiff and unwilling, after an hour or so, loosened up and in the rhythm of it, it seemed to Tom Cloud that he could go on chopping like this forever. Sweat leaked down off his bare shoulders and tickled his back. Small chips scattered in the air around him, sticking to his belly, his face, in his hair. Needles scratched his arms, leaving trails of white in his darkening skin.

The trouble was, once he was chopping and his arms and hands doing their work without direction, his mind was free to trot off in any direction like a pony turned loose in a grassy pasture. And so he thought about the girl. Her face and figure, her lips and how they'd kissed him back, her words and how they'd lifted him up then dropped him back. He thought in circles, hope adding strength to the axe, doubt taking it away. Two weeks of it, almost. Twelve days to be exact, and they had enough cedar cut and stacked and Tom had thought about Maria too much. Or so it seemed, because his thoughts led around and around and he began to see that his life had been

171

taken out of his hands. That idea caused him to stop in mid-stride and catch his breath.

Is that what he'd done? Put it all in the girl's hands? His hopes and plans not his any longer, everything waiting for her to decide what she wanted?

From the other end of the log they were carrying Lanny said, "You plan to stand here all day?"

He shook his head. "Ain't a good way to live."

"This thing's heavy, Tom. You need to save your meditation til we put it down."

The cabin had two rooms. One for sleeping and one for all the rest of living. It had a fireplace of smooth rocks hauled out of the creek and a fieldstone floor laid over the bare ground. It was chinked with clay they'd mixed with dried grass. It smelled like a cedar chest inside. The roof was tight and rainproof, made of shingles split from short lengths of log and held in place by the nails Lanny had remembered to buy.

And there was more. A shed beside the horse pen for feed and saddles and such, a three-sided shelter inside the pen, a two-holer outhouse, and another construction behind the cabin with a wide door that swung shut on iron hinges and could be called a barn if you had to call it something.

"I'm tired," Lanny said.

They'd both cleaned up and put on fresh clothes, the day's sweat and dirt washed on down the cold creek. "Me, too. The worst is over, though. It's a real homestead now."

"You need a smokehouse." Steaks off a fresh-killed yearling buck were frying on the hearth. This was the first fire they'd built on it. "Not to mention the chicken coop you had in mind a while back."

Tom laughed. "There'll always be somethin' else, I reckon. This bench will do to sit on for now, but I'd like a couple of storebought chairs, too. For company."

Lanny swallowed some coffee. "How you plan to keep them people from burnin' you out again?"

"I guess I don't know the answer to that." The question had

172

come up more than once in different words and was at least as worrisome as the girl. He'd thought about taking it to the sheriff, but then Tom himself had gone against the law when he'd torched the Loup place and shot that pony down. The law, such as it was, would surely side with an old-time rancher like Loup against him.

"You may be wrong about that," Lanny told him. "John Thurman is said to be a man friendly to these German settlers, and that might mean he ain't all that friendly toward people like Loup. I know he ain't friendly toward rustlers, 'cause I stopped at the sheriff's office to talk to him about it. He likes proof to back up accusations, but they've held a few hangin' parties hereabouts."

Tom located some plates and dished up the steaks and some boiled pintos. "Remind me to get a dutch oven. Man's got to have his biscuits."

They ate sitting on the single bench, side by side at the split-log table. The meat was tough, the way fried venison usually was, but it tasted good to tired men at the end of a long day. They could hear the sound of birds in the bushes outside and the barking squirrels finishing the day's quarrels. "Somethin' else I'll remind you of is about them squirrels. They gonna eat your pecan crop."

Tom sighed and swallowed a mouthful of meat. "I got a while yet."

"It may take poison to get rid of 'em all."

He'd thought about that and had put it out of his mind. "No, I don't want to do that."

"Well, I ain't sayin' it's a good thing. Just maybe the only thing."

He shook his head and kept quiet. The beans could've benefited from some fatback. Always something else to do, something else to think about. This was a different life from the one he'd expected a few years back–a life among the gambling crowds of big cities, no responsibilities except to put his opponents on their backs and collect the winner's purse. Now it was smokehouses and pork and squirrels and most of all, a

173

pretty girl he wanted more than anything.

CHAPTER 42

She spent some time on instruction. "You know the coop, now? How you build it?"

"I do," Tom told her. "Already built and waiting." The smell of manure and chicken feathers and grain filled his nose.

"Every night you close the door so the wild animals can't get at them. And the owls. Everybody wants to eat the chicken." She laughed and he thought it made her look younger. For just a moment he could see a girl inside the aging face of the Schneider woman. "And one wing always trimmed. It grows out, then the chicky flies away over your little fence."

"Yes, ma'am. I'll raise 'em right, you don't have to worry." For want of anything better, they'd cut air holes in four feed sacks and stuffed their unhappy pullets inside. The half-grown rooster had a sack all to himself. The sacks hung behind their saddles, feathery heads poking out of the holes and making noises that caused his mare and Lanny's gelding to pull against their reins wanting to get away from it all. Tom had another sack tied off at the saddlehorn, with three cabbages from the Schneider garden. "You should put in a kitchen garden, too," she'd said. "The vegetables you must have."

Ward Dobbs rode past them with three men following. Dobbs raised a hand in greeting. The others paid no attention. Lanny spit out the snuff he'd carried for most of the morning, opened his canteen and washed his mouth out. He raked his lips clean with his teeth and spit again. He grinned and said, "The only time them boys think about a chicken is when it's piled on a plate."

An hour or two before sundown they had the hens and rooster unloaded and pecking at grain in the new pen. The birds didn't seem happy. Tom didn't feel all that happy, himself. He knew that sometime in the future there'd be eggs for breakfast and maybe a fried drumstick now and then on his table, and it would be worth the effort. Right now, though, he was tired of the whole business—his hands scratched and bleeding from the frantic kicking of the young birds and his ears tired from all the clucking and squawking of the afternoon.

Lanny didn't appear to be happy either. "I can see why most of us choose cattle raisin' over chickens."

Tom found the energy to smile. They washed in the creek and took care of the horses while blue jays and mockingbirds fought in the agarita bushes.

It always made him feel good to walk inside his new cabin. Something about it was more than just shelter. It seemed like a part of him now, his effort caught and reflected back from every log, every stone. All that work and sweat turned into a lasting thing that he, and Lanny, too, would always be part of. He put kindling on the grate and laid two logs on it. "I think cornbread would go good with that cabbage." No comment from Lanny. He looked over his shoulder. Lanny hadn't followed him inside.

"Tom." From just outside the door. "You better come back out here. And bring your Henry."

He counted six men on horseback coming up from the south. Militia? He didn't see Grant. They rode two abreast, heading straight for the cabin. Behind them a two-horse buggy made slow time over bumpy ground. Another animal carrying an empty saddle was tied behind it. Two figures on the seat, looked like a man and woman.

He said to Lanny, "Why don't you go behind the rock fort over there?"

"I'd as soon stand right here."

"I know you would, but you can back me up better from cover if you need to."

"I guess you're right. But just so you know, if you get yourself killed I'm takin' them danged chickens back to that little woman."

He thought three of those faces might belong to the riders

who'd chased him into that blind canyon. The buckboard driver was Loup himself. And beside him the woman from the porch. His wife, Tom figured, the mother of Phil Loup, who trotted his horse beside them.

Tom raised his rifle. "Stop right there!"

The six riders reined their mounts in and pulled their own saddle guns, but the buggy kept on coming. He let it.

The team halted. The buggy rocked back and settled. The woman stared hard at Tom. She wore a cloth bonnet on her head, but it was plainly her. Loup looked at her and said, "This the man?"

She gave him a slight shake of her head. "I don't think so." She looked away from Tom. Loup kept staring at his wife, but he spoke to Tom.

"She don't think so. But I do, and three of them men back there think so, too." He turned his head and focused hard eyes on Tom. "I come here today to ask you straight out. You the man torched my place?"

"Let me ask you straight out, you like my new cabin?" Loup didn't look at the cabin and didn't answer him. Tom went on, "You the man torched the old one?" Tom recognized a sound, a quick metallic snap, a settling into place, a gun hammer cocked and ready to fire. A voice.

"I done it for him." From behind him. It was a voice he'd heard before. He turned.

They'd come up behind Lanny and had him on the ground. So, no help after all. The man walking toward him was the Crenshaw he'd seen riding with Phil Loup. One of the rustlers back on the Bigboy. The other man standing over Lanny seemed familiar, and Tom remembered the razorback at the bar in Mason.

"That man is healing up from a bullet wound. Go easy on him." Lanny didn't move. He was bare-headed and still. Tom guessed they'd knocked him in the head. Maybe killed him, after all.

The others had spurred forward and dismounted. There were smiles now that the danger had passed.

Crenshaw pushed his pistol barrel under Tom's hat and lifted it up, scraping its sharp edge into his scalp, hurting. With his other hand he reached over Tom's shoulder and took the Henry. Loup got down from the buggy. Phil Loup walked up to Tom and slugged him in the belly. Tom bent at the waist, his breath gone.

"I told you it wasn't over."

Two of the men dragged Lanny closer to Tom, his boot heels plowing shallow trails in the dirt. When they dropped his arms he groaned. Alive, anyway. For now. A knot swelled above his right ear.

Tom stayed bent, fighting to get his breathing back to normal, waiting for the spasm to ease. He heard the old man tell somebody to unhitch his horse from the buggy, then yell to the woman.

"You go on back home! And feed the team when you put 'em up."

Crenshaw said, "He's got some good looking stock in his pen back there. Good trade for the one he shot."

He remembered the crazy mare they'd shot for sport the day they branded his hip. "You already killed one of mine." It came out weak. Phil Loup brought the barrel of his rifle across Tom's face, ripping the skin of his left cheek and knocking him to the ground. When he opened his eyes he saw Lanny's face just a few inches away. Blood seeped into his mouth. He could taste it. Well, they had the upper hand again it looked like. And there'd be pain and maybe death because he'd been careless and let it happen. He deserved it maybe, but Lanny didn't. He heard the old man again from a little distance.

"This one ought to burn real good. Wood's still green. That sap'll go up easy." He could hear the smile in the man's voice, the smug sense of power that couldn't be overcome.

So this is how all that work and hope ended. Flame and ashes. All of it for nothing.

The woman had known him, of course. For reasons of her own, she hadn't said so, but it made no difference. Loup had come here to finish things. Burn it all, take the horses and anything else he wanted and leave two bodies behind. He rolled over onto his back and sat up, then forced his shaky legs to stand. His face was numb. A dull ache spread into the bones of his jaw and across his neck. He spit a clot of blood. He looked at Phil Loup.

"Let's me and you fight square." He said it loud enough for all of them to hear.

Phil switched the butt of his rifle around and was about to punch him with it when the old man spoke out.

"Wait a minute, son. What'd he say? He wants to fistfight you?"

"That's right," Tom said, wiping blood off his cheek with his left hand and then onto his pants leg.

"Like sort of a duel?"

"He likes throwing punches at a man that can't fight back. I wonder how he'd do in a square fight."

Loup came close. His face took on a look that put Tom in mind of the times the Schneider woman had called him a wolf. Teeth showed behind tight lips. A bead of spit hung in a corner of his mouth. "You sayin' my boy's a coward?"

"We can find out. Point your guns somewhere else and let me fight him." It hurt to talk.

The look of cold hatred became something else. Appetite, maybe, a look of hunger. "Phil ain't ever lost a fight to nobody."

"He's got nothin' to worry about, then." Tom kept his eyes steady. He wished to be anyplace but here. In any situation but this one. Only good thing—he felt no fear. Resignation, though, he felt that for sure. All he could do was stretch this out. Win or lose, these people would kill him and Lanny. They'd burn the cabin, the barn, all of it. No choice, though. You do what you can with what's in front of you. This was all he had, and even this not settled yet.

"What do you say, son?" Loup's narrow eyes never looked away.

"Save us a bullet, I reckon."

Loup grinned like a young kid. This was making him happy.

179

"When Phil whips a man, he whips him all the way down. You understand me?"

"I believe I do." Tom turned to the younger man and said, "You're sayin' he'll beat me to death." He got the words out before Phil Loup brought his right fist out of nowhere and sent Tom sprawled across the still unconscious body of his friend Lanny Tarver.

CHAPTER 43

Everything came down to what he knew, what was a part of him. The fight. The man shucking off his gunbelt and his shirt and coming back at him with the others patting his back and handing out words of support and sure belief. Not the old man, though. No, he stood back with his arms folded and a smile on his face, a father who had just given a present to his son. Pride rode the smile, and satisfaction, and that strange look of appetite.

Tom shook his head and got his eyes focused, then rolled to his knees in time to catch another punch that glanced off the side of his head. He ignored the fuzziness it left behind and stood up, got his guard up and began to circle to the left, staying away from Phil's powerful right hand. He needed a little time to get himself back together, his breath back in his body, his instincts in line. If this man got him on the ground, Tom had no doubt how it would end. He'd never stand again. This was a fight to the death.

The watchers yelled at him to go on and fight. They wanted blood. His blood. From the corner of his eye he noticed that Lanny had sat up. Maybe not hurt too bad, he hoped. But no help to Tom. He had no weapons, and the look on his face said he was still working his way back.

Phil came at him again, plain murder in his eyes, both fists pumping. The man was all power and hate, and he could hurt an opponent, all right. No doubt he had hurt many. This sort of attitude didn't stay home and sit on the porch. It went out looking for a victim.

It had been a while since he'd faced another fighter, except for the angel in disguise, who hadn't been much of a match. It came back to him fast, though, the moves, the concentration, the narrow tunnel that closed him in with the other man. All at once the familiar quiet settled on him. All the sounds, the yells from the Loup riders, the fussing of horses, even the birds in the agaritas, vanished and it was just Tom and Phil Loup in that place he'd been so many times. Phil dropped his left hand and exposed his face. Tom sent a left jab into it and his shirtless foe rocked back and stumbled. Loup fell backward, catching himself on his elbows and lurching to his feet again. Tom knew if that happened to him, he'd never make it back up, but he stepped away and let the man get himself together. This match was all that stood between him and a death by hanging or rifle shot, or burning. Whatever else the crazy Loups could think up. He wanted to keep on stretching it out, making time.

That quick jab had been solid. Phil's right eye had already started swelling. A few drops of blood creeped down from his nose and stained his lips. And it had made him mad. Before, he had seemed to almost be playing at it, like a cat with a mouse.

The man's entire body became a weapon now. He barreled into Tom swinging rights and lefts that glanced off, none of them hurting much and easy enough to dodge. Tom planted a hard right fist into the sweating belly and felt it sink almost to his wrist. And that would have been all the fight if he'd stayed in after it, because Phil was going through the same thing he'd done to Tom. Only worse. He was hurt and couldn't breathe. He swung around facing the other way, his mouth gaping open.

And again Tom backed off and let him recover while the men circled around them yelling out encouragement to their boss. A quick look at the old rancher still standing with his hands folded and that same smile on his face. All at once Phil spun and lunged forward, jamming a shoulder into Tom's middle, shoving him back, and back farther, and finally down to one knee. Couldn't go down, couldn't let it happen, it would be the end of him, it would mean boot heels and pain. He remembered that day and what they'd done to him, and it kindled a heat that filled him up with a new strength born of anger and hate. He grabbed the boot coming at his face and lifted, pushed hard and had it in the air and the fighter on his back again in the dirt.

Phil started to rise and got himself nearly upright, but this time there was no backoff. In Tom's mind there was no thought, no calculation. It was all turned loose now, everything that held him back, that held him in. Half-standing, off balance, Phil took a hard blow that snapped his head back and left his mouth bloody and uncertain. One second, two, three, Tom waited for the man to get himself oriented and when he did Tom went for him again.

Fists and flesh. Blood. Sharp splinters of pain. All of it spinning around him like a tornado, and him in the dark middle of it, a blind killer who could not stop. He hit and hit and hit again and then his hands stopped moving. He stopped moving. Other hands held him, pinned him tight and close.

He waited and the world came back

They had him, the watchers, two men on each arm and somebody behind him with an elbow knotted at his throat. Breath came fast, cutting at his throat like a saw, and not enough air at that, because he'd run himself down. No feeling in his own hands. Phil Loup down there twisted and still. Unconscious or dead. It didn't matter.

Tom tried again and again to pull loose, but they held on until they'd brought him to a stop. And when the stillness came into him all of his strength poured out. He could not have lifted a fist just then. Nor spoken a word. A deep weariness settled into him. Breathing easier now, he waited for whatever was next.

The old rancher walked toward him, the smile gone now, glancing down at his son and walking past to stand just inches from Tom. "I guess you whipped him square, I'll give you that, but it don't make no difference."

Tom looked for Lanny and met his eyes. He was staring at Tom in a way that had a grin in it despite everything. The knot on his head had swollen bigger, but the banty rooster in him was awake again.

"You men hold this squatter tight." He walked away and came back with a coiled rope. A noose was already tied in one end. It's what they'd come here for. He held the big coil up and the smile came back. "One of them pecans got a limb that's just right. I tried it out already on one of your dutchy friends a few years back."

He dropped to the ground, knees first, and made a try to catch himself before his face plowed into the dirt. His hat rolled away. The coiled rope had fallen from his hand. Beside it was a feathered shaft. A blunt arrow.

CHAPTER 44

Tom felt the suffocating arm release his neck. They let go of his arms. He spun around and popped a right fist into the face of the rustler Crenshaw. Another body on the ground. He reached for the arm holders, but they were already retreating from him.

A blunt arrow? The boy? Loup was getting up. The projectile had stunned him, that's all. He was conscious and looking for a weapon. He found Lanny Tarver instead. Lanny stood waiting for the best angle and when it came he planted a sharp toe into Loup's head.

Tom saw Crenshaw's helper climbing onto a horse, the others already mounted and circling with their rifles out. The rancher was on his belly, shaking his head, and Lanny stood ready for another kick if it was needed.

Crenshaw tried to push himself onto his knees, but Tom put a foot onto the small of the man's back and shoved him down again. Somebody yelled and the Loup woman was there in her buggy pulling her team to a halt. She was off the buggy before it stopped, with a whip in her hand. Her horses breathed hard. Her face was set in hard lines, not a woman's face at all, but it was only a mask that fell away when she dropped the whip and knelt beside her son.

More clatter. More people. It seemed to Tom that the very air around him had taken on life and sound. Loup rolled onto his side and tried to pull his pistol, but his wife saw the movement and grabbed his arm.

Her voice was soft, almost apologetic. A woman accustomed to taking orders, not giving them. "That's enough," she said. He looked at her with the same hatred he'd shown Tom.

"You know better than that."

185

She ignored him and pulled the gun herself and handed it up to Tom. Tears tracked her face, and she seemed not plain at all just then, as if she had remembered who she had once been.

The Indians? They were climbing off a horse-drawn wagon. Sage, with a new crutch under his arm, the women, the boy carrying his bow, reaching down and picking up the arrow he'd used to stop Loup. The priest? Tom felt like he was dreaming. It was Father William, all right, with earnest things to say to the men, standing in the midst of the milling ranch hands, all of them uncertain, unsure what Loup wanted from them now. Another robed man sat on the wagon seat, holding his work team still.

"You men have done enough harm," William was saying. "I'm telling you in God's name to leave here. Now."

The razorback rode up close and leaned down to him. "You don't give the orders, priest."

William grabbed his shirt collar and jerked him out of the saddle. He lay there stunned long enough for Tom to react. "Lanny, I believe that's the man shot you."

"You sure?"

"Yeah, it's him."

Before Lanny could make a move William raised his hands as though to push him back. "Wait, now. No more of this, please. Everybody calm down."

Under his boot, Tom felt Lynn Crenshaw twist away, and before he knew it the big man was up and swinging a fist at him. Tom saw the flash of clenched teeth deep in the heavy beard and sent a right cross that came from far back, sending him down to stay.

But Crenshaw's crony was on his feet with his pistol out and plainly ready to shoot. He said, "I'll finish the job this time." He fired at Lanny, but William threw himself in front of the banty and took the bullet instead. The force of it spun William to the ground.

Tom was one step too late to stop it, but he grabbed the pistol with his left hand before the man could fire it again, and swung the butt of Loup's heavy sidearm into the hate-filled face. The blow had been hard enough to kill, and Tom thought maybe it had.

The Indians stood beside the wagon looking on. On the wagon seat the driver raised a Winchester and levered a shell into the chamber. He pointed it at nobody in particular. He said, loud enough for everybody to hear, "You don't think I'll shoot, then pull another gun." Nobody did.

The shot had left Tom deaf in one ear. He bent down to the wounded priest and opened the man's robe. The bullet had torn into his upper right chest and punctured a lung. Red foam rose and fell with every breath. He said to the Loup woman, "It's in his lungs, a sucking wound. Need to get him inside." He could barely hear his own voice. To Lanny, "Help me lift him."

The bullet had torn a big exit hole, but at least it wasn't inside him any longer. They stripped his upper body and rolled him onto the bunk. He was unconscious and fighting for air. Tom said, "Miz Loup, I'm way short on medical supplies here. You know the Schneider place?"

"Yes." She looked away, her voice softer than he'd expected. "I wouldn't be welcome there."

"He'll die if we don't get him bandaged up. May anyway."

Lanny said, "I'll go. Charley's faster than that rig."

"All right. Hope she's at home. I know she'll want to help with this."

As Lanny went out the door the two Indian women came inside. Sage's wife carried a big white cloth. Not a flag of surrender, though. She'd brought it to use on William. He'd cared for them many weeks now, and they began to return that care with tenderness. A wadded strip of the cloth went into the sucking wound, and the bigger portion into the crater on his back. They kept him turned on his side and held the cloth in place. He seemed to breathe easier.

Tom walked outside just in time to see the rear end of Lanny's gelding disappear into the trees along the creek. It would take time for help to come. He hoped it would be soon enough to save the life of that man on his bunk. A very brave fellow who'd likely saved the banty rooster's life.

The second priest still sat on his wagon seat and still had his rifle pointing vaguely at the quiet Loup riders. Two men were still on the ground—Crenshaw and the razorback. The old rancher had managed to get Phil Loup into the two-horse buggy and was climbing up beside him.

"That's my pistol in your hand," he said to Tom.

"I'll give it to your wife."

His grin was nasty. "I doubt she'll come home."

"And I wouldn't blame her."

The rig began moving away. The riders fell in behind it. Phil sat with his head between his knees.

"What about your friends here?"

Loup looked back at him. "Sounded to me like they're rustlers and killers. Ain't no friends of mine."

CHAPTER 45

It was full-on dark by the time Tom figured out the best thing for the Apaches. He opened the barn and made them understand they could spread their blankets there for the night.

The second monk had dismounted from the wagon and knew their language. He relayed Tom's words with a calmness that failed to reflect the violence of the past hour.

Tom told him, "I got enough on hand to feed all of you tonight, sir. My house is crammed full of folks, but you're welcome to rest here with the others."

"I'm Matthew," he said. He had a deep voice and a look of toughness about him. "If William lives until morning I plan to carry him to a doctor. And these men—" he gestured toward Crenshaw and his friend, both sitting with backs against the barn wall and their hands tied—"should be delivered to the sheriff."

Tom had half expected to find the razorback dead from the heavy blow to his head. The man was confused and quiet and a fist-sized knot grew where he was hit. Able to stand up for hanging, maybe. Lynn Crenshaw paid no attention to the movement around him and had nothing to say.

Matthew said, "If there's room for me, I should go inside and say last rites for William."

"I think them heathen women will pull him through."

A sad laugh. "Still, it has to be done." He looked around at the Apaches, the men with their hands tied. He sighed out a long, despondent breath. "I broke a vow tonight."

Tom waited for the man to go on, but he stood silent after that. "Well, sir, I expect you saved some lives. I hope you'll think on that."

It was nearly dawn when Lanny came back with the Schneider woman and Ward Dobbins. The woman looked tired, her hair loose from the night wind. Lanny told Tom, "I'll put their horses in our brand new corral and hope the black don't take offense."

Inside the cabin Matthew knelt beside the bunk working a string of beads through his hand. He'd sent the Apache women and Sage away to rest as best they could inside the little barn. On the bunk itself Father William still breathed, his heart still beat. Matthew looked up when the door opened and then shut. Light came from a flickering lamp in a corner, joined now by the lantern Ward Dobbins carried.

"Ah, Cara, thank you for coming."

"How is he?"

Matthew moved back to make room for her. She opened the black bag she carried and began taking out the medicines and bandages from it.

Tom stepped outside, leaving the nursework to the others.The Loup woman had stood up from the bench she'd been sitting on when Cara Schneider came inside. She followed Tom out the door and walked away toward her buggy. Daylight was not far off, but it was still plenty dark around him. He heard, and then saw Lanny coming back from the corral, a shadow inside the darker shadow of night.

"That William feller still with us?"

"He is. I suspect he'll get through this if we can carry him into Mason to a doctor."

"Where's the redskins and the rustlers?"

"In the barn. Crenshaw and the other one's tied up. They may try breaking loose, but the boy's got his eye on 'em."

"We need to elect a mayor soon as everybody's up. This place is growing fast."

"Well, I'm hoping not everybody's permanent. I never got a chance to ask why they brought the Indians back here. I didn't expect to see them again."

Lanny said, "It's a good thing they showed up, though. Otherwise I think me and you'd be dancin' on air right now."

190

"Why don't we slip in the barn with all them other folks and try to get a nap in before daylight. I'm pretty sure it's our last chance for a while." Lanny followed him to the door. It smelled stale inside. A dim lantern made shadows on the walls. Nobody slept. Every eye was open, but there was no talking. The two men still sat in the same spot, their hands tied. The young Apache boy sat watching them. Sage lay flat on the ground, his head supported by a rolled up blanket, the crutch beside him. The two women stood still, waiting for the new day.

Tom heard the door open behind him and turned to see the Loup woman. She looked lost and alone. He stepped closer to her. "Come on inside, ma'am. We're crowded, but you're welcome to find a spot to rest."

"Thank you. It's warmer in here. I thought I'd just sit in my buggy, but I got chilled."

"I appreciate you helping us out last night." He glanced down at his swollen hand. "I'm sorry about everything. Your boy."

"My son is like my husband, a bully and worse. I don't blame you for what's happened."

"You can just tell me it's not my business, but you got anywhere to go? Someplace to stay til all this business dies down? It worries me, the way your husband was talking."

"You think this was something new? This is how he's talked and how he's behaved for as long as I can remember. I've wanted to leave him for years, but I've been afraid to do it, afraid he'd chase me down like he threatens. Kill me. Like he's killed others. The boy who owned this place before you. The husband of that woman in there. I don't even know how many. And he's taught my boy to be just like him. No, to your question."

"Ma'am?"

"No, I have no place to go. I am the most alone woman on earth."

The last of her life force seemed to leave her with those words. Tears formed in her eyes, reflecting fragments of light from the lantern. Her despair seemed a solid and real thing and it felt to Tom like a heavy weight had entered his own body.

191

"However it seems, I assure you, ma'am, you are not alone. I offer you my personal guarantee of that. Don't know how just yet, but there's a way to help you out, and we'll find it. You hold on and we'll find it."

She picked a place and sat down, leaning back against the wall and closing her eyes. Lanny Patted Tom on the shoulder and said, "A world with you in it is a better place, but I hate to see you spread too thin. You can't solve everybody's troubles, much as you want to."

"Yeah, I know." Talk died down and there was silence around them, the sound of heavy breathing, and from the corral the stomp and fuss of horses. No sleep to be had.

Minutes went by in the silent little building. Maybe a half hour. Tom could bear it no longer and went to the door, Lanny following close behind. Gray light surprised them both. Not the sun, not the rosy red of dawn, but the first hint of it. Enough to see by, enough to say it was day again.

A figure stood outside the cabin. It was Ward Dobbins. He drew on his smoke and it lit his face for a second. They went over to him. Tom said, "How is it in there?"

"No good." Dobbs drew on the roll of tobacco again then dropped it and stepped on it. "He quit breathing a little while ago."

CHAPTER 46

Tom hadn't expected it. He had it worked out in his head how they'd take William to a doctor and get him well. How this whole mess would sort itself out. Now what? He turned and found Lanny had walked a few paces away and was standing with his back turned. "Lanny?" No comeback, a silent shake of the head. Tom walked around him and looked into his face. It was barely light enough to see the tears.

The little man's voice was no more than a whisper, barely heard above the morning breeze. "He died saving me. I don't know if I can stand it." He took off his hat and walked toward the horse pen.

Cara Schneider came out, carrying her black bag. "Father Matthew wants to take the body back to the mission right away." There had been tears, but they were over now, and her face reflected the hard knowledge of what had to be done. "Can you help him, please, carry dear William to that wagon over yonder?"

The Apaches must have sensed what had happened. They added to the small group around the wagon, Sage hobbling on his crutch, the Loup woman with them. Before he climbed into the seat Matthew found Tom. "We haven't talked about the Indians. They wanted to come back here and we were on the way when we met the lady and she told us what was happening."

"What am I supposed to do with 'em?"

"The chief there told us the white lawmen gave them to you. I never was clear just what that meant. If you can't handle it I guess we can work it out later. Move them to the reservation, maybe But right now I have other problems to take care of. Can they stay with you? They got nothing. The flood took all they had."

"No, you go on with what you need to do. They can stay. For now, anyway."

Matthew turned away from Tom and raised his voice. "Missus Loupe? It may be best if you come with me to the mission for now. We can give you shelter."

Cara Scheider stepped forward, still holding her bag of medicines. "I was hoping she might come home with me today. There's plenty of room in my house, I make very good tea, and there are things John Thurman needs to hear about. Things she can tell him." She turned to the silent woman. "Would you?"

"I...I don't know. I'm so ashamed. I don't know what to do."

"Leave your buggy here and ride behind me. We'll go and get some sleep and everything will seem better then." A quick nod. She put her arm across the slumped shoulders and they walked away. Tom went behind them, watching for Lanny and not seeing him.

Ward Dobbs caught up and they got the horses ready. As he helped the ladies mount up Tom said, "That Father Matthew be okay you think? He's got a long trip."

Cara Schneider said, "I think so. He was once a wanted outlaw. A hired gun. A very tough man indeed. He'll be all right."

Another surprise. "Well, I heard him say he broke a vow. Picking up that rifle, I guess."

"Probably. But we forgive him, don't we. Surely God does, too."

After they rode away Tom looked around for his friend again but still didn't see him, and wondered where he'd gone. Best to just leave him alone, probably. It was the kind of thing nobody ever expected. He'd seen it during the war, of course, a man sacrificing himself to keep another man alive. You didn't expect it, and when it happened it left you with feelings that had sharp edges and took their time working through you. He opened the barn door and went inside and Lanny was there.

His .44 was pointed into the face of the fellow who'd killed William, tried to kill Lanny twice. Nobody was saying a word.

Both prisoners had their heads down, staring at the ground. The pistol was cocked.

"It's a bad idea," Tom said. "I understand how you feel, but you shoot this one, then we have to shoot the other one, and then we got to lie about it. I won't feel good about it and doubt you will, either."

No reply.

"Well, I'll leave it to you. I have to go see about our Apaches." It didn't bother Tom to leave. Let 'em sweat. He figured Lanny would decide against it. If he didn't it was no loss to the world.

Part of his mind listened for the boom of Lanny's pistol. The rest of it paid attention to the small band of Indians who bunched outside his cabin door now. These people didn't show their feelings, but he knew how they felt, anyway. How they had to be feeling. No home, no possessions, two of their bunch dead in the river flood. Well, he'd opened his mouth to the militia back there, made the offer, and he was a man who kept his word. He'd keep it now. He walked up to Sage and held out his hand. The Indian took it.

CHAPTER 47

These whites—all whites—were hard to understand. His people, the Lipan Apaches, fought the Comanches, fought any outsider who threatened them. Fought the way night fought day. Two things. Two peoples. One against the other. But these people were not separate that way. No, they spoke the same language, wore the same clothes and you couldn't tell which ones would shake your hand in peace and which would kill you.

The Jesus man, though, that one who died, was a good one. Brave and quick to save aother man's life. That one who died would take you sick and hurt and put you in a bed. Would give you medicine and feed you and make you well. And after all of that ask nothing from you. A man like that was honey on your tongue, and an empty place inside you when he was gone. Like Yellow Bow, lost in the river.

And now, this one. This fighter. Sage shook hands in the white way. The Apache felt ashamed. They had come here like beggars. His leg was mending, but not yet whole. They had no horses, nowhere to go. Could not travel back to Mexico yet as they had meant to do. Could hardly even feed themselves. For the others, he would feel the shame and endure it, and ask this one for help. Ask such a thing for the first time in his life, and of a white. He would rather cut his own throat, but for the others he would not. He would ask.

Tom Cloud didn't understand what the Indian was saying. He called. "Lanny! Come out here. I need you."

The barn door opened and Lanny was sliding the big pistol back in its holster. He paused, blinking his eyes in the new light, then walked over to stand beside Tom. "What?" He was breathing in that shallow and careful way a man did when he was working his back to the present moment after combat.

"Ask this man what he was telling me."

The telling took a while and Tom felt like he could go to sleep on his feet, he was so tired from the night.

But it ended like all things do and Lanny said, "You ain't going to like it much, but what he is saying, long story short, is he's putting his soul and the souls of these others in your hands. Go easy, now. It's a delicate matter."

Lanny was right, it was a delicate matter and he could wound this man badly right here in front of his family by acting poorly toward him. So, instead, he nodded his head and reached to shake hands again, and with that he guessed he had made a contract he'd have to live up to.

Tired as they were, it seemed best to haul the two prisoners to Mason and let the sheriff there decide what to do about them. The men's horses were loose and standing beside Tom's pen. Attracted there, he supposed, by the other animals inside it.

They left before noontime. He'd showed the Apache women the food stores in the cabin. He'd have to bring back more. The boy could bag some squirrels with those blunt arrows of his, and they left the Henry behind for Sage. "Tell him it's a loan, though. Don't want no hurt feelings later when I take it back."

Lanny grinned. First time since that episode in the barn. "They don't comprende loans. I just told him it's there if he needs it."

And before they left Tom made sure to thank the boy, the skinny little Indian kid who'd very likely saved his life with one of those arrows. When Lanny explained Tom's words the boy bowed his head and smiled with pleasure. It was a good thing to be brave and even better to be told you were brave, but he had not meant to smile.

"This is the worst trip I ever took," Lanny said when they were a couple of miles from Mason. "All these horses to keep in line, and them two murderin' rustlers for company. It's a blessing we're about done with it."

"I'm glad you held your fire back there in the barn."

"Yeah. Well, I don't expect I ever meant to shoot. It was just fun to think about it."

A deputy went after Thurman and brought him back to the jail from somewhere in town. He was a medium-sized man with a plain face under a stained hat. He seemed neither friendly nor unfriendly while he listened to their story. Just seemed to take it all in without a reaction.

When they were done he said to Lanny. "I think I talked to you a while back, didn't I? About this very thing."

"Yes, sir. That ugly one is the one shot me. The other one is his partner in crime, though. And there's a brother loose, too. Don't know his name."

"That would be Ezekiel. Everybody calls him Easy. But he ain't."

Tom said, "What do we do now? I need to get back home with a load of grub."

"I'll need to talk to Miz Loup. And that other fellow from the mission. What'd you say his name is?"

"Matthew is what he told us. But I heard he used to be somebody else."

Thurman chased a smile off his face and said, "I know who you mean. A genuine miracle, if I ain't mistaken."

It was plain they'd be late in the night getting back. They managed to feed themselves at a corner cafe and went on from there to the general store. They'd brought the stallion along to serve as packhorse, and he didn't like the job. He fought the lead rope. Town wasn't far behind them when Tom decided he'd had enough of it for the day.

"I'm tuckered out," he said.

"Yours truly is in the same shape."

"Why don't we bivouac at that little creek up ahead?"

Morning came too soon. The fire was out and Tom was shivering from the dawn cold when he raised himself from the dream.

It had been about the girl, he could remember that much, and so real he could smell her hair and feel her lips on his. He reached an empty hand to his mouth and shook his head to clear the last rags of night away. It was morning and time to move. But Maria had taken over his thoughts and he couldn't go another day without sight and sound of her.

They made coffee, and over the rim of his cup Tom said, "I got to ask another favor."

CHAPTER 48

Lanny had tried his best to talk him out of it, but the scent of her hair wouldn't leave him alone. He'd ignored his friend's good sense and his own instincts and there was the Weiss house, just in sight now, and the new corn crib he'd helped build. Why was he there? Simple enough. He had to see her. Had to. It was an unexpected thing and the fault of the dream. And so he'd sent Lanny Tarver down the road alone, leading the black horse loaded down with the things they'd bought in town.

Now he began to wish he hadn't come. There was more than dreams in the air. Even the Appaloosa mare felt it. She kept shying away from every noise off the trail, throwing her head when he reined her back. Not like her. And not like himself, either, to come hat in hand this way. A beggar asking for crumbs. He couldn't stop himself, though. He pushed on.

A dog barked somewhere back of the house. Before Tom could climb the front steps the German man came outside, letting the screen door slam behind him. He seemed friendly enough, but there was something on guard in the smile under that cottontail mustache.

Tom took off his hat and said, "I'm sorry to bust in like this, but I was hoping to visit with your daughter a few minutes if you'll allow it." The boy, Tobias, came out the door and stood beside his father.

Florian Weiss said, "Oh, sure, if she was here a visit would be fine. But she is not, so me and my son will have to do, I guess."

For the first time, Tom noticed that both of them looked dressed up. The big mustache was trimmed. Tobias had combed his hair. "I'm imposing on you, I reckon. You look like you're about to go somewhere." Inside him an ache began. Not a physical pain. It was deeper than that and hurt more, and it had to do with his feelings on the road here and Maria gone. Gone where?

"There is a wedding," Tobias said, looking away. Tom felt the solid earth shift, as if it meant to suck him down to some dark place. He tried to speak and couldn't do it. The air around his head seemed thick and filled with sound that he could almost, but not quite, hear.

The boy held something out to him. "Maria told me to give you this."

What had he said? Tom felt his hand reach for the envelope, felt his hand take it. The air was filled with more of that sound he could not hear. He looked down at the thing in his hand and up into the eyes of the man and boy. Their eyes pitied him, as a beggar is pitied. Anger flashed through him and quickly died. He felt it in the tips of his fingers and in his legs and feet. The air turned thin and quiet.

"I'd best be getting home." He put his hat back on. "Good day to you both." They were silent, but as he headed south he heard Florien Weiss call out.

"I'm sorry, my friend."

It took almost the entire ride back to town before he could make himself stop and open the letter. He dismounted and walked a circle around the mare as he read it.

My Dear Tom Cloud,

I should have said this to you in person, but I have not the courage. And you might have changed my mind if you tried hard to do it. So, yes, I am marrying another man and that will be my life. I think it will be a good one. You must make your life with someone else. I hope that it will also be a good one. I am very sorry if I have hurt you.

The ink of her signature was blurred, as if a tear had fallen on it. Tom felt the ache explode into hot anger and loss. He wadded the envelope and paper in his fist and threw it into the brush beside the trail. He untied his horse and climbed into the saddle and started down the road to Mason. He would never understand it, but that made no difference. People acted in ways that made no sense, and he thought maybe Maria herself didn't know why she was doing this. It wasn't up to him to change things, though. It was over and done. A hundred yards farther on he turned the mare around and rode back. He got down and crawled under the brush to where the crumpled letter lay. He took it back and opened it and smoothed the paper out, then folded it and stuffed it in his shirt pocket beside the pigging string he still carried but never thought about.

He stopped in Mason long enough to mail a short letter to his mother in Tennessee.

CHAPTER 49

A tipi stood beside the creek. The canvas Lanny had hauled from Mason covered the poles instead of deer or buffalo hide, but it would do for now. Lanny must have understood that Tom's visit had not gone well. He said nothing about it, and asked no questions. A pot of stew simmered on the fire beside the tipi and Sage's wife brought him a bowl of it. He had forgotten to be hungry, but it had been nearly an entire day since the cafe in Mason. The stew was hot. He blew on it to cool it and ate a spoonful. It tasted good. He ate all of it, then went to the pot and filled the bowl again.

The girl stayed in his thoughts for days, try as he might to think his way around her. Married and in her own house by now, he figured, and gone out of his life for good. It wouldn't stop hurting. Now and then he paused in whatever he was doing and took out the wrinkled note and read it again. After a while the words of it lost their meaning, if they'd ever had any for him. But that blur on her name, the tear she must've blinked onto the paper as she signed it, stayed after him. If it made her sad enough to cry, then why had she done it? The log cabin no longer felt the same. It was just a place to sleep now, not a place to make a home in.

They built a smokehouse, and Sage had improved enough to lend a hand. He still had to use the makeshift crutch when he walked, but the leg would take some of his weight now and Tom thought it wouldn't be long til the man was whole again. The boy and his arrows were hard on the squirrel population. He was a dead shot and usually harvested two or three every morning. Tom and Lanny brought in three white tail deer and the Apache women butchered them for hanging in the smokehouse. Meat for winter. The weather had turned colder and Tom got out his canvas coat but he didn't wear it because Lanny hadn't brought anything for cold weather and it didn't seem right to work warm when his friend couldn't. The Indian women crafted ponchos, such as Mexicans wore, for themselves and the other two, out of the blankets Tom had bought for them.

"I hadn't expected to have so much fun and stay so long," Lanny said.

"We can go up to Mason and buy you a coat. Anything else you need. It's the least I can do after all the work you've put in here."

Lanny thought about it and finally shook his head. "I told Rudy I'd be back to ride that line you probably remember well. They'll be counting on me to show up like I said I would. All my belongings is still there. I just pray to God they don't team me with Francisco. He don't talk, and I do, which would make for a long winter."

He didn't name a day for leaving, but Tom felt alone already. The Apaches were there, of course, but he wouldn't even be able to talk to them once Lanny moved on. Funny how a man could go from happy to mournful in the blink of an eye, and all because of what somebody else thought or said or did. Didn't seem like a good way to live, and the only way out of it seemed to be changing himself. There ought to be something you could rely on besides a pretty girl's favors. There ought to be something hard as flint in a man that nothing could break. And he'd known men like that. Had they gained from it? He didn't think so. And he didn't think he truly wanted to be one of them.

So if you were Tom Cloud and you wanted to make it through life without the pain of it, what did you do? Despite all the thinking, he never solved the question. Nor, he supposed, had any man.

He was in the horse pen trimming the stallion's hoofs the day John Thurman came to visit. Another man rode beside him—a deputy, from the star on his shirt, a taller and younger man than Thurman. "Good day to you," the sheriff said. Both men got down and tied their horses to pecan saplings close by. Tom finished his work and came out of the gate. Thurman shook his hand and pointed to the deputy. "This here's Micah Jennings, Mr. Cloud. We been over to the Crenshaw place talking to Easy concerning your complaints against him. Your friend still around? The man got shot?"

"Yes, sir. He's inside. Claimed to be cooking something to eat for dinner, but I can't swear he was truthful."

"I see you've got the Apache clan situated."

"They're doing all right, I think. No trouble to have around, and I'm starting to get used to the idea."

"The man looks like that leg's about healed up."

"Yes, it is. Why don't you come on inside? This close to noontime you're bound to be hungry and Lanny puts together a pretty good plate."

"We've got to get on to town, as inviting as that sounds, but I could use a quick cup of coffee while we talk. How about you, Micah?"

The deputy laughed. "You know me, Sheriff. I like my coffee."

They brought their cups outside. Thurman had some questions for Lanny.

"If all this comes to trial can we have you back over here to testify against the two I've got in jail?"

"I'll be ridin' Bigboy line pretty soon. I expect they'd turn me loose long enough for it, though. Billy Barnett would be glad to know he won't lose any more cows to 'em."

"I don't know if we can get a conviction on rustling. They deny it, of course. Easy, too. But we've got good witnesses to what went on here just now. People saw what happened and heard what was said. Miz Loup, in particular."

"Yes, sir. All you have to do is let me know and I'll try to be here."

Micah Jennings spoke up. "There's another reason we stopped off to talk to you."

Lanny sipped at his coffee and waited.

Thurman said, "Ezekiel Crenshaw ought to've been drowned at birth. Since nobody did us the favor, you need to keep a close watch out for him. He talks like he'll find a way to keep you out of the witness chair at his brother's trial.

"You don't have to worry, Sheriff. He won't stop me."

"Just wanted you to know, that's all. Some of these outlaw characters are mostly talk, but old Easy is a bad man, from his toenails to his ugly bald head. Don't turn your back on him. You, either, Mr. Cloud. He mentioned you, as well."

"What about Matthew? Or whatever his name is. The church fellow I told you about. He saw it all, too."

"We've talked to him." Something made both Thurman and Jennings smile.

Jennings said, "I don't think we need to worry."

Tom said, "Must be a good story there somewhere. I'd like to hear it."

Thurman laughed. "You're right about that. Just figure that old Easy knows who not to mess with."

CHAPTER 50

Sage sat on the ground with his back against one of the big pecans. He could do the work there and let the leg rest. It had been hard with the crutch walking through the woods. He'd spent a long time looking for a mulberry tree, but saw none. Mulberry made the best bows and it's what the Lipans had always used when it was available. But cedar was good, almost as good. He began to shape the limb with his big knife. It would take a long time to make it right, but he had time. And little else. His hands did all the necessary work, accustomed to it, shaving the wood, letting the thin slivers pile up. It would be good kindling for his woman's cooking fire. His mind stayed free and wandered backward and forward, remembering and hoping.

The bow would be a gift for his son, along with arrows tipped by flint. And with the new bow, a name. The boy had saved his life and done it bravely when the river almost killed him. Sage had not yet decided the name, but it would come. The flint for the arrows was already chipped and shaped. He had only to walk along the creek and pick the old arrowheads up. The white man had a big can full of them. He'd seen it. And the old flint would be a gift from people long gone, from before this time. Such a gift would make the arrows strong and swift.

Lately he had dreamed of the place of the rainbow, that country he had wandered in his head when the fever had him. Always then he had been alone, but in these new dreams someone else was there. Two others were there. One was the white man. The fighter. Sage had seen his face plainly. The other was only a shadow, but he came along just out of sight, a dream within a dream. It seemed to Sage that the shadow moved like his old friend Yellow Bow. And maybe that's who it was, in these nighttime travels. Beside that shadow that might be Yellow Bow walked a smaller shadow, and one held the other's hand. Over all of it that rainbow. That strange, curving rainbow.

The two women wondered about corn. This was a different situation, not one they were used to, and it was hard to know the right way to behave. But Sage had nearly died, and while he was a man and thus the maker of decisions, the asker of questions and the one who answered them, he was not back in himself yet. Part of him was somewhere else. It would return, there was no doubt about it, but for now the women wondered about things and asked one another about them. Corn was one of the things they wondered about. They knew the tall man didn't understand them, but the little one spoke Spanish and so did they, and it was a way to ask things and tell things.

"We've been wonderin' what to do about the squirrel population, and I think maybe them Indians would be a help to you. Poison free."

They had a blaze going in the fireplace. A couple of small cedar stumps and some pecan limbs dried out and gathered off the ground. It was past time for some serious wood chopping and a stack of firelogs close to the cabin.

"They want to plant that pasture out yonder with corn come spring. It's what they always do when they settle. Feed the horses, feed theirselves. Makes 'em feel at home. Of course they're not at home and they know it, but the corn would make 'em feel better about things, so I'm supposed to ask you about it." He spit a brown stream into the fire. His lower lip was rounded out from the wad of snuff it carried. Tom sat puffing on his crooked pipe and stayed silent, listening. There was some wind picking up outside, crowding smoke back down the chimney and stirring it around. The wind whistled with a lonesome call as it felt its way along the roof edge then went on by. Tom thought about the Indians, hoped they were warm in their tipi.

"You need to get 'em a hoe or two and some seed. They'll do

it from there. And what you'll get out of it will be first some feed for your horses, maybe a little for yourself, and most important, you'll create a diversion tactic."

"A diversion tactic."

"That's right. Like we used in the war. Once that corn is up and growing good all them tree rodents will head for it. They may cut the crop back some, but I think it'll spare the pecans a bit. Don't you?"

Tom thought about it. "You're right. Sounds like it would help us all out. Even the squirrels."

The morning Lanny rode off toward the Bigboy Tom tried to keep the heavy lump out of his throat. Already in the saddle, Lanny said, "Anyway, I'll be back for that trial if they ever get around to it."

"If I ain't here you feel free to stay anyway, long as you need to."

The little man took off his hat and leaned over the saddle horn. "You plan to leave? You never said anything about it."

"I'm going up to Tennessee for a while. See my folks. I wrote 'em to look for me in the springtime but I may not wait that long."

"So that pretty girl is over with? You never said."

"Yeah. She's over with."

It was true. Tom had never talked about what happened to the girl. *Maria.* Her name always sent something cold and hurtful through him. And Lanny had not asked.

"You plan to catch a boat from Galveston?"

He'd thought about that. "No, I believe I'll take my ponies. Both of 'em. Ride one and use one for a packhorse."

The silence thickened, like water reaching toward a boil. Lanny stayed watching him, finally sat the hat on his head and tilted it down and touched a boot heel to Charlie's flank. Tom listened to the sound of the horse's hoofs until he couldn't hear them any longer. Birds were in the agaritas fighting over the last shriveled berries of the season. He heard the quiet running of water from the creek. Far behind him the Apache man sat against a pecan tree using his knife on that long piece of cedar.

211

The Apaloosa mare and the black racer stood in their pen side by side, their necks hanging over the fence, watching the empty place Lanny had left when he went out of sight.

CHAPTER 51

How long would the ride to Nashville take? He had no idea, but now that he had made up his mind to do it, he felt a sort of excitement at the prospect. There'd be new country to see, new people along the way. He began to believe he'd go sometime soon, not wait for spring. He imagined his folks' surprise, how his mother would head for her kitchen, saying he was too thin. Saying he needed some good cooking. Travel toward his old home in the cold of winter seemed a welcome thing as he lay in his silent cabin for long nights wishing life had taken a different turn. A week after Lanny left for the Bigboy he saddled the Appaloosa and paid a visit to the Schneider place.

Ward Dobbins said, "It's funny you'd ask. We was just talking about that the other day."

"Well, I may take off pretty soon on a trip to Tennessee. I need both of mine, so that leaves them without a way to get around." He'd come across Dobbins and two other men at the same sheep pen as the last time through here, doing some work on the pen. A half-dozen rotted fence poles lay on the ground beside new ones just put into place.

"Give me a few minutes and I'll come to headquarters with you. I believe we've got a pony would suit you."

He was a gray, probably fifteen or sixteen hands high, a gelding that acted a little wild when Tom tried to get a hand on him. Dobbins laughed. "Everybody hates that danged horse. Your Indian chief may not appreciate him, neither."

Tom remembered his crazy mare, her unreasonable ways, her killing. Rudy Sterns had said almost the same thing about her the day Tom left the Bigboy living in a black cloud of despair that he thought would never go away.

Ward Dobbins said, "I'll rope him and put him in the corral

by the house so you can get a close look at him. He's sound, though. You won't find anything wrong with him except he's mean. While I'm doing that, why don't you go on to the house and talk to the missus about it. She'll have to be the one to quote you a price."

"I don't guess there's extra rigging around, is there?"

"Not that I know of. You can probably find something at the livery in Mason wouldn't be too expensive."

At the door he felt a dread of going inside, where he had seen Maria last, sitting at the table drinking tea. Dreaded the possibility that Cara Schneider would talk about her. Ask him questions, maybe. Or worse, tell him things he didn't want to know.

He asked for a price on the horse. She tried to have him sit down for tea.

"No time for it, ma'am. I need to get up to Mason and look for a saddle." And he didn't want to sit at that table just now. Maybe never. The Loup woman was still there. She looked better, a quick smile crossing her face now and then, and seemed to Tom a younger version of the person he had first seen on that ranch porch a while back.

Cara Schneider said, "You have time to sit. I give you the horse. Okay? You do so much for those people, so I can do a little if I may. I give you the horse, and what else is I have a saddle and bridle for you, too." She lost her smile. "It was my husband's. It has hung there all these years and nobody has touched it since the day he died. I think that I wanted it to be ready in case he needed it again." She laughed and the smile came back and stayed. "Silly old woman, huh?"

It surprised Tom. He was used to paying his way. Gifts didn't come along much in his experience, but this was welcome, and he said so. "That's good of you. It gets me and the Indian out of a tight spot."

"So sit."

And once he did, once the cups of strong tea were ready, it wasn't so bad after all to think of Maria as she had been in this place.

"How long will you be gone?" Cara asked him over the rim of her cup.

"Don't know. It's a good ways off, and I'll want time to visit with my folks."

"You will come back, though?"

Would he? What was here to come back to? A lonesome cabin that hadn't seemed lonesome before, some trees and a creek. The ashes of that old fire he'd used to burn the loup brand off his hip. Some homeless Apache Indians. The memory of a girl he'd wanted for his own, and lost. The old heaviness spread itself in his throat and chest. But he said what she wanted to hear.

"Yes ma'am, I plan to."

The Loup woman had been silent, sipping at her cup of tea and listening. When she spoke up it surprised Tom again. He'd gotten used to her silence. Her voice was deep, almost like a man's. "I want to thank you." She paused a long time. Maybe that was all she had to say. She rounded up her thoughts and went on, "The day you came to burn us out." It sounded bad, the way she'd said it, but he could see it wasn't meant to accuse him. He felt bad enough already about what he'd done in that fit of anger. "When you came to the house you meant to go inside with it, and you didn't. Because I was standing there, I think. Because you recognized innocence despite the guilt of what my husband had done to you."

"Burned my place, you mean."

She nodded her head and raised the cup to her lips, sipped at the tea and put the cup down. "That. And the other."

"What *other* is that?"

"Oh, I know. I always knew. He bragged to me of it."

Tom reached into his shirt pocket and took out the pigging string, leaving the wrinkled sheet of paper. He tossed it on the table between them.

"They tied my legs with that," he said. "I've kept it since. I thought I would tie Phil's legs with it, or your husband's. Give back what they gave me. I won't. I'm done with all the crazy feuders. It never was something I wanted part of, and I'm tired of it."

"Yes. And so am I. I have talked to a lawyer in Mason. I will make a new life for myself. Philip is a grown man. He can choose to stay with the dark half of his inheritance or follow me to something better. And that is what else I thank you for. When he fought you, and you didn't kill him with your fists. As you could have. As he would have done to you. As maybe he deserved."

Cara said, "It would be a sorry world if everybody got just what they deserved, wouldn't it. Without forgiveness there is nothing."

"I didn't forgive him," Tom said. "I just didn't kill him."

She smiled and said, "You will. One day. Forgive him, I mean. Now we have to talk about Maria."

A clock on her fireplace mantle struck the hour. The vibrations of it seemed to *pierce* him, as she had said that day, amplified by the sound of the name. What he had dreaded.

"Don't believe I can."

"I know you cared for her. And she for you."

"Makes no sense. Why would she do it?" And there he was, talking about it, when he had not meant to do it. Not even his own tongue belonged to him these days.

"She is young. It was what her father wanted. Florian Weiss persuaded her to marry a German man. He thought it best for her."

"I can't see why. And it's been mighty hard on me."

"Yes." She pointed at his cup. "Drink your tea. It's very good. Time will pass and you will forgive what has happened. You will find a new life that you don't imagine now, and you will be glad again."

"But why didn't she talk to me about it? Why didn't she tell me?"

"You could have changed her mind. That is why. And Florian Weiss wanted her to marry a German man."

"Makes no sense." He turned his cup in circles on the table. His arms felt weak and something burned behind his eyes.

"Life is like that. You will forgive it."

"I doubt it."

"Oh, not today. But one day."

"Why do you think so?"

"Because without forgiveness, there is nothing."

Maybe the woman was right. She'd lived longer and been through more than he had, so it could be she knew more. But not today. What he needed right now, what felt better, was his sense of betrayal, and anger at it. It was a kind of shield and he kept it in place. The cup was still half full, but he'd had enough. Enough tea, and enough conversation.

"I better go round up the horse and rigging." He started to stand up, but Cara touched his arm and stopped him.

"When you come *back*," she made the word almost two words, emphasizing it, like she read his thoughts, "when you come back Sonia Loup here may ask you to speak to her lawyer about the things that happened." She nodded her head at the Loup woman, who turned to him and said, "If you will."

He wanted to go. "If you want me to, I will. It's a rough thing, him pushing you out of your own home."

"It is my home, all right, my land, my cattle. I will be pushing *him* out soon. The other way around." Another surprise.

She smiled again. It was good to see, made her almost pretty. "I was married before, you see, long ago. We built that house you didn't burn. We stocked the ranch. My husband died a year after Phillip was born, and later I married the man you know. He turned hard and strange after a while and made my son like himself, and I let it happen, though I was never sure how. No, it is mine and I will take it back. He is the one who will leave."

217

CHAPTER 52

The Apache boy rode the gray to a standstill, the big horse blowing hard, then walking in circles, the boy letting the reins slacken against the arched neck. Tom stood beside Sage watching it happen. He could see pride in the man's face. The boy had been as brave as you could ask, climbing into the saddle while the horse shied and reared, threatening to buck. Then the wild run that came back toward where they stood, and the boy off now, holding the reins, and the gelding, still breathing hard, behaving himself. The boy laid the reins in his father's hand. Sage set his crutch on the ground and put a foot in the stirrups. The leg was still weak and it looked like he wouldn't be able to lift himself to a seat.

Tom stepped up, the boy, too, and they hoisted the big man onto his new horse. There was a shine in the Apache's eyes and on his face. Something good to see. It took the gray half a minute to understand that his new rider was like the other one, only heavier, and stronger. And someone he could not defeat. He stopped his craziness and answered to the reins, as he knew he must.

Tom had made the mistake of going to Mason after he left the Schneider ranch, for the hoes and some seed corn. The gelding, on a lead rope, had fought him the whole time, and the ride home had been a tiresome event. The two Apache women had been happy when he handed it all over, though. It was worth the trouble to see them glad, even for a little while. One more thing done and now maybe he could get ready for his trip. He had already decided to leave the Henry behind for them to use. His Peacemaker would be enough arsenal for the journey.

Sage wheeled the horse and nudged his flank and rode him away at a trot. Out of sight of the others he slowed the gray to a walk. The fighter was a good man. Maybe somebody to trust. It was a puzzle, though, him making gifts of the horse and saddle, and handing over the rifle. Sage had nothing he could give in return, and that made him sad. From the man's signs and the few words he had understood, a journey was being planned. Somewhere far. What was to happen now for him and his people, his family? Could they stay here beside the water and be safe, or would others come and tell them to move on, or even worse? He wished for a way to speak with the fighter so that he could understand the things that were happening.

When he saw the wagon coming he thought at first it was the one he and the others had ridden from the mission. But no, it looked different, and it was pulled by two mules, not the horses the robed men used. Two men rode in the wagon seat, and in the rear of it two women and two children. And yes, one of the women, the old one, it was her. The curandera, who had fed him bitter water and sent him off to that distant rainbow.

Closer now, in the back of the wagon a man rose up and braced himself against the side slat. A man who lifted a thin arm into the air and made a fist with a bony hand. A man lost in a wild river and come again into being at this unexpected time and place.

Yellow Bow.

And not only the man, but the boy, as well, one of the children who rode the wagon. They lived. Not in a dream. Not *only* in a dream. Here, on this solid ground, among rocks and trees and grass and the running stream. They lived.

The gray reared under him, and he let it, keeping his seat, keeping his feet in the stirrups, leaning forward til his new mount settled and kicking now into a gallop, meeting the wagon that hauled his lost friend. Sending whoops of joy into the countryside, finding what he had believed forever gone. In that rolling wagon, and in himself, as well.

Tom came to see what all the laughing and talking and turmoil meant. And there were his friends, the people who had nursed him when he lay close to death that long time back. And

220

the other one, the man, why that was the one they called Yellow Bow. Back from the dead, looked like, and his little boy, too. No wonder the good times and happy faces.

The old woman watched him as he approached. She nearly smiled to see him. And the girl. She was there, too, unchanged and shy when he said hello. From the wagon they had unloaded sacks of provender and a fresh-killed white tail deer, and it looked like a feast was in the making. Time to celebrate, he figured, and why not?

Next thing he knew, the Mexican man, the guitar player, had grabbed his hand and was shaking it and patting him on the shoulder, smiling big and looking pleased. "You well," he said, "You strong. Good. Bueno. Good."

The old woman said something to the girl, who hurried over to him.

"Mi abuela say ask you is all right that we come for pecans again."

"You tell her, you tell all your family, it is all right today and tomorrow and ever more for you to come for pecans. As much as you want, whenever you want. You tell her that."

It took a little while, and the girl turned to him once like she'd forgotten some of it, then remembered and finished telling it and ran back to the frolicking boys.

The translated words made the old woman smile. The first one he'd ever seen on that wrinkled face. She joined the women at the cooking pot, the fire under it just now blazing up. Smoke hung in the air and made it all seem better, the people, the talking, the friendly faces and even the tears in the eyes of the women. Almost like home. But he knew better.

He was out of place among them. They talked in words he couldn't understand, lived lives separated from his own. The girl's mind was on play, and it was hard to get her attention. Even harder to keep her still long enough to ask a few questions. But he learned the little she knew about the finding of the Indian man and boy. Wandering on foot across the hill country, hungry, dazed by what they'd endured, discovered by a sheep herder and brought to the mission. Begging to come here after Yellow Bow learned where the others were.

Tom stayed around until the food was ready and ate with them. He thought it would be wrong to go off by himself. An insult to these people, really, when it was a glad time for all of them. He managed a hand shake with Yellow Bow, telling him in words the man plainly didn't understand, that he was glad to see him again, alive and well.

That night, alone in his cabin, he tried to sleep and felt lonelier than ever with the talk still going on at the Indian camp, their excitement too high to calm, loud enough to find its way to him through the night air and the log walls. The guitar, its strumming low and almost lost among the other sounds.

Hours later, while he lay there trying not to think of Maria, quiet took over. The Apaches and the pecan gatherers wore themselves down and settled in to rest. He could imagine how good it must feel to the woman who had thought herself widowed to lie beside her husband again, to feel once more safe and cared for after being alone and grieving for man and boy lost in that wild water. There was no sound now but the familiar noise of insects and tree frogs, and he felt himself drift off into sleep.

It seemed only seconds later he woke up to light coming in the window and the cold muzzle of a pistol pressing into his forehead.

CHAPTER 53

He'd seen that face once before, around a branding fire the day Lanny Tarver nearly died. Now he could put a name with it. And here he'd been foolish enough to disregard the warning from John Thurman, leaving his door unlatched and offering unobstructed entry to Ezekiel Crenshaw. Thinking the man was making empty threats that would never come to pass.

Tom had heard it said many times that by middle age you've got the face you deserve. Ugly thoughts and ugly deeds showing. And this was an ugly man, his hat pushed back and his bald head shiny in the morning light. His beard was shaggy and untrimmed. His breath carried the scent of onions and grease. His eyes were dark slits of threat and one of his front teeth was missing. Tom turned his face to the side, trying to escape the nasty breath.

"Don't you be moving, now. 'Less you plan to die right this second."

"What do you want?" It came out a whisper, the first words he'd spoken in hours.

The man laughed. The sort of laugh you expected from that sort of mouth. "What do you think I want?" Tom didn't try to answer him.

"I want you not sayin' another word against me or my kin, is what."

"All right."

Another laugh. "Givin' me your word of honor, are you? Well, it ain't near enough."

"I'm about to head for Tennessee." This was pretty strange, he thought. He didn't feel any fear, though he knew this fellow was likely to shoot him. He wasn't begging for his life, and he was not really bargaining for it, either. Just handing out simple facts.

"You'll be back, though."

"Maybe not." As he spoke he saw in the edge of his vision movement at the door, the unlatched door he'd left open to any danger that cared to come in. There was no sound.

No sound at all until Easy's gunhand jerked away from Tom's head and a great moan bled out of that battered mouth. And Sage was there with another plunge of his big knife, this one into the exposed neck, and in a wink man and gun collapsed to the floor. This was a heck of a way to greet the day.

The Indian wiped his knife on the dead man's shirt sleeve and slid the blade into the leather sheath on his belt. He bent without a word and took hold of Crenshaw's feet and pulled the body out the open door leaving a bloody smear on the new stone floor.

Tom got up. The stone was cold under his feet. He avoided stepping in the blood trail. Something he'd have to clean up now, but at least it was't his own blood. He was pulling on his boots when Sage came back inside.

"Friend," he said, pointing a finger at Tom. And again he said, "Friend," pointing the same finger at his own chest.

The body waited for him when he finished dressing and walked outside. Under a tree not far from his door. Sage had left it there and gone back to his camp like murder was a normal start to his day. Of course, it was not truly murder. The Apache had done it to save Tom's life, or it seemed that way anyhow. It would surely sound like it when Tom recounted the story to Thurman. He'd make sure of that. On the other hand there might be a better way to handle the situation. The sheriff and deputy knew this character was out looking to hurt people. There was a time when visitors got themselves shot or hung with no questions asked when they came calling the way this one did.

Tom rolled the man over and checked his pockets to see what he was carrying. They were empty. If he'd had money it was gone. So was the pistol and cartridge belt. Oh, well, Crenshaw didn't need any of it any longer and Sage did.

Now here came the Indian again leading his barebacked gray. Yellow Bow walked beside him, looking better this morning. A good night's rest and a couple of good feeds had filled him out a little—put some spunk back into him. They picked opposite ends and lifted the body and laid it over the horse's back.

Trouble broke out.

The horse reared up, jerking the bridle reins out of Sage's hands and took off at a dead run, Easy still on his back, hands and arms flopping. He was still there when the horse went into the trees across the creek.

It was the middle of the morning by the time Tom brought the gray back. He'd ridden his Appaloosa mare in the chase, figuring the gelding might head back toward Schneider's, and so circling in that direction. Sure enough, he had found the runaway standing as calm as you please in some brush with the reins so snarled in the undergrowth he couldn't get loose. Easy Crenshaw was missing, though. Tom guessed the body had to be somewhere between the two points, and when he reached his cabin the body was back under that same tree with the shirt and pants nearly ripped off.

Sage and Yellow Bow had gone searching on foot.

The two men set out to accomplish the maneuver that had failed on first try, but this time borrowed Tom's lasso and tied the horse to a strong tree first. While they were at it Tom found the Mexican girl and brought her with him. It was not entirely clear to him just what Sage planned to accomplish once Easy, or what was left of him, was tied down good on that uneasy animal.

"They go bury him," she said, after a short conversation.

Tom thought about it. He ought to go and report this. What would happen after that? Would it make trouble for Sage or for himself? Probably not. Then again, when you thought about it this was mostly a private matter. The man had come killing and got killed, and that was that.

He'd about made up his mind on it when they untied the gray and began to lead him off. Tom said to the girl, "Ask 'em where they're headed." Sage called back an answer to her, but didn't offer to stop. He seemed to be in a hurry. For good reason, Tom thought.

"To bury that dead man, is where."

"No, no, no." Tom trotted after them and took hold of the reins. "Now wait a minute." The procession halted. He motioned to the reluctant girl, who wanted to be somewhere else, and she came over to them.

"I understand the buryin' part. *Where* is it they plan to bury him. That's what I want to know."

The answer was quick. "Only Sage and Yellow Bow will know. You are free of it."

That sounded good. And it wasn't going to make any difference to Crenshaw. It'd probably come back to haunt him later, but taking this story to the sheriff was just going to make trouble for everybody. Well, the Mexican family would head back south, and the Indians wouldn't be talking. He remembered the smell of Crenshaw's breath and the feel of the gun muzzle against his head. "Bueno. Okay. Go." He waved them away and dug a coin out of his pocket and put it in the girl's hand. She wasn't used to money, but he made her take it.

He spent the morning cleaning up the cabin and packing the things he'd be taking with him to Tennessee. Seemed like the trip had already started in his mind, and part of him was headed off in a northeast direction while most of him stayed put getting his chores taken care of. He made sure to gather up a big sack of pecans. His mother would get a kick out of making a pie with them, hauled all the way from Texas. The squirrels, the Mexican family and the Apaches, too, were stowing away this year's crop, or part of it, anyway. The crop was lots bigger than the harvesters could handle. Most of the nuts would hang in the trees or lie on the ground til they dried away to nothing.

It seemed a great waste to him, to let that happen. Of course, it had been happening every year back to a time before men began counting years. Or pecans. One more wouldn't matter. Or two. Would he come back to this place? Was it home? Like he told that man this morning, maybe not. Maybe it never was.

226

CHAPTER 54

Sage watched the fighter ride away on the back of his big black horse, the Appaloosa mare on a lead rope loaded down with packs for the journey just now beginning. Not the usual time of day to begin traveling, barely past the middle of the day, but for reasons Sage didn't understand, the fighter was anxious to be gone. The horses walked with a lively step and the fighter himself seemed not as sad today as usual. Starting on a journey was like that—it always made you expect something better just ahead. They'd put the body of that bad man in a place nobody would ever find. No one would know what happened here this morning.

He had not yet gotten used to the fact that Yellow Bow was alive again, and every time he remembered it he could feel a little rise of happiness in his chest. Beside Sage stood his son, the boy with a new name now that told about what he had done that day at the flooded river.

The fighter had opened his house to them if they wished it. The other building. The pen for his wild gray beast. Had left them some of the white man's money they could use for food if they needed it. But he and his family would stay in their tipi. It was what they were accustomed to. And in the wikiup they were building beside it. With the long rifle he would hunt the game that had always fed them. They would plant corn in that field over there when the weather warmed. That was how Apaches lived. Not in houses. They'd have the eggs from those hens, too, and maybe one of the hens sometimes. After the corn grew up and they had made the harvest, maybe it would be time to cross the border, but not yet. If that time came, he would know it. He wondered when the fighter would come back to this place.

And the family of pecan-gatherers paused in their work to watch the young man go. He had come to them again and made it clear that they were always welcome here any time they wished. He was a very different man than the one they'd found near death that other year. And generous with his land and trees they had learned he owned, paid for with money from his own hand, and with papers to show it as things were done now. The old curandera watched while pretending not to watch. She felt an interest in the young man, as she felt for the Apache, as she always felt for those who found their way back to life through the things she knew and the things she did not know, but only believed.

Cloud rode all night, running from memories, and made camp the next day on the Brazos not far from the Waco settlement, a long way above the ford he and Lanny had crossed coming out of Houston after their ride on the riverboat *Mary*. His heartaches were behind him in the limestone hills and along those rivers and creeks he'd known for many a long month. His hopes, too. Back there. He ate cold bread and beans for his supper and thought about Maria, not wanting to. Knowing he would never find an answer to it, and the knowing added to the tiredness of the travel. He slept. And he slept well, without dreams, and felt better when morning came.

He ignored roads and well-traveled ways, heading in the general direction of Tennessee, on a northeast diagonal across Texas that led him past the growing town of Dallas and across the Trinity river, and two days later it was Texarkana at the border.

The ride through Arkansas took enough days that he lost count and didn't know whether it was a Monday or a Friday or something in between when he came to the wide Mississipi river with Memphis just a ferry ride away. He watched the rolling river and remembered how he'd felt on the deck of that paddle-wheeler coming down from St. Louis sick and afraid. The horses had behaved well the entire trip, had been no trouble at all. He'd stopped a couple of times where oats or corn were available and restocked with enough to keep them fed.

Somewhere in the middle of Arkansas he had surprised himself, realizing he hadn't thought about the girl in a day and a night.

He stayed two nights in a Memphis hotel, or most of two nights, leaving it behind in the early morning of the third day. He and the two horses had reached the town tired and needed rest.

This was pretty country. Cold country. Colder than it had been in Texas. He rode east and then began edging to the north, not far from Nashville now and the farm, feeling at home, seeing the country he'd known all his life as a boy and then as a soldier. Nashville and the area around it had about recovered from the hard fighting that went on there and healed up some, with more healing to come. There'd been way too much death amid cannon fire all around that place.

By the time he got close to the end of his trip he was feeling even stronger anticipation of seeing his mother and his father again, seeing the farm again where he'd helped plant and harvest, smelling the air of it, seeing the look of it. He couldn't stop now and camp. Couldn't pause in his quickened pace, the mare trotting forward with no interest in slowing down, catching excitement from him. The black stallion began to act up, and Cloud didn't mind a bit.

CHAPTER 55

Then there was only one more bend in the sandy road and he went past the big walnut tree that stood at the edge of it, where one of their plow horses had reared up and thrown him off, a long time back. He'd been what then? Ten? Twelve? Remembering it made him smile. And there sat the house. Just like it had always sat and like he had never been away from it.

Somebody saw him a long way off, because he heard a faint shout and figures appeared on the wide front porch. The house was unpainted boards and batts like most houses in the young countryside. But it was well-kept with a fence around it and grass growing inside the fence with a pretty walk from gate to porch, made of flagstones he remembered gathering out of the field. His mother had always made it a point to keep grass growing around the house. Something a lot of people never thought about, much less worked at. And it had a steep-pitched roof of corrugated tin that was rusty in spots. Up under that steep roof at the top of stairs was where he and his brother had once slept. The loft had been overly warm in the summer, being so close to the tin roof. But the tradeoff was that it stayed warmer in the winter months, the heat from fireplace and stove drifting up to keep him company. It was nice to see again, the place he'd grown up. The place he'd left to go fight a war, then left again to fight bare-fisted in alleyways for money. Seeing it again caused him to think of his brother and wish him still alive, wish the Yankee bullet had missed its mark.

There were four people on the porch waiting for him. He waved, and they all waved back.

He was riding the black that day and the stallion was showing himself off to the people watching. A new sort of prance that Tom had never seen before. Well, why not? Tom felt like prancing, himself. He was home, and he felt like he could sleep for a week.

His father's handshake had not lost any of its grip. He looked about the same, maybe a little softer at the edges, a little grayer, but the same strong and eager man Tom had always known. It was a relief to see him like that, to stand next to him and notice the familiar assurance and humor that had always peeked out of the man's clear brown eyes.

O'keefe was nothing at all like the boxer he'd faced in that St. Louis alley. He was very thin and a leg dragged when he stepped forward to shake Tom's hand.

He said, "I'm glad to see you," but that's not how the words came out. He sounded like he talked through a mouthful of something. Tongue-tied and slow.

"Same here, Pat. I'm very sorry what happened to you. But I'm glad you pulled out of it." A quick picture of Easy Crenshaw and the gun at his head those several mornings back flashed through his mind, and a sense of guilt. Maybe he should have gone to John Thurman about it after all. He shrugged off the thoughts.

His mother put her arm across the young woman's shoulder and said, "This is my very dear helper and friend, Suzanne."

"Call me Suzy, please. Everyone does." She didn't look the same, either, as she had that day he saw her last. That day she had been all fear and sadness, looking up at him facing the hard loss of her father.

Today she smiled at him. Her long hair was a kind of blond leaning in the direction of strawberry. Her skin was tanned from working outdoors here on the farm. Her body was slender, but not skinny, well-formed under her long dress. Her voice carried a little of the irish lilt, which surprised Tom. And charmed him. He wanted to hear more of it. A few seconds of silence went by and he realized he was staring at her.

"Sorry." About what, he didn't know. "I'm kind of draggy from all the miles. Guess I'd better see to my horses."

"They are beautiful horses," she said. "Especially the black.

I'd love to ride him sometime if you'd let me." He wanted to say to her that she was also beautiful, and she was, but this was no time for saying that sort of thing. Still, what was happening to him? It was the trip, the long ride. He was tired. Tomorrow he'd be better. All he needed was some good food and sleep.

"I would. I mean, I will. Anytime you want."

His mother hugged him again and said, "I'm so glad you're home." And what he thought when she said that was that this house was a wonderful house and his family was a wonderful family, but his home now, his grown-man home, might be in another place beside a running creek in a grove of tall pecan trees. It was confusing and he was tired.

"So you go on and see to your horses and the two of us will fire up the stove. I'll bet you're hungry."

"You'd win that bet. I'm near starved." He started down the steps.

His father said, "Hold up and I'll go help you. We'll turn 'em into that pen down by the barn." O'Keefe found one of the rocking chairs on the porch and sat down in it.

They unloaded his packs off the mare and brought them to the porch, then Tom led the black and his father took the Appaloosa's lead rope and they headed for the pen.

On the way Tom heard himself say, "That girl, that woman, I guess, is she—is anybody courting her?" He tried to make it sound casual, but it didn't.

The brown eyes looked a little more amused than usual. "No, son. They've been around, all right, but she don't seem to take a shine to 'em. Not to anybody yet." He laughed. "I'll tell you the truth, and I'm serious about it, I think she's been waiting for you."

www.ingramcontent.com/pod-product-compliance
Lightning Source LLC
Chambersburg PA
CBHW070616130626
46556CB00001B/380